D1644980

WICKED WHISPERS AT ST BRIDE'S

DEBBIE YOUNG

Boldwood

First published in Great Britain in 2022 by Boldwood Books Ltd.

Cover Design by Lawston Design

Cover Photography: Lawston Design

A CIP catalogue record for this book is available from the British Library.

Paperback ISBN 978-1-80483-051-2

Large Print ISBN 978-1-80483-050-5

Hardback ISBN 978-1-80483-049-9

Ebook ISBN 978-1-80483-052-9

Kindle ISBN 978-1-80483-053-6

Audio CD ISBN 978-1-80483-044-4

MP3 CD ISBN 978-1-80483-045-1

Digital audio download ISBN 978-1-80483-047-5

Boldwood Books Ltd
23 Bowerdean Street
London SW6 3TN
www.boldwoodbooks.com

For my grandma, who taught me Scrabble and so much more

Played well, games should make generous winners and gracious losers of us all.

— MISS HARNETT, HEADMISTRESS OF ST BRIDE'S
SCHOOL FOR GIRLS

It is a wise father that knows his own child.

— WILLIAM SHAKESPEARE

— THE MERCHANT OF VENICE, ACT II, SCENE II

1

THE DIE IS CAST

Steam fogged Mavis's glasses as she poured a cup of coffee for each of us at Old Faithful, the geyser-like coffee machine in the school staffroom.

'I reckon the bursar put Hairnet up to this board games malarkey,' she said. The geography teacher for St Bride's School for Girls paused to clean her glasses on her baggy grey cardigan. 'He'll try anything to justify turning down the thermostat. He'll assume the girls' body heat will keep them warm as they huddle together over card tables all afternoon.'

Hairnet, or Miss Harnett, to use her proper name, had proposed 'this board games malarkey' for this term's essential life skills programme, which she had announced to us just an hour earlier at our staff meeting. Mavis began a surprisingly good imitation of Hairnet making her speech.

'"The aim is for the girls to learn as many board and card games as possible",' she said serenely, with the confidence of one who makes the rules. '"More importantly, they should learn the art of gracious winning and losing. Besides, what better preparation for a wet weekend in a country house, or being confined with illness or even being shipwrecked on a desert island?"'

'Provided you're lucky enough to have a compendium of games wash up beside you on the beach,' put in Oriana, the maths teacher, as Mavis carried our cups and saucers to the table in the middle of the room where I was writing in my planner.

I took a grateful sip. The warmth of the coffee was very welcome after half an hour in the draughty hall for the first assembly of the term. At least the staff were allowed chairs, unlike the poor girls, who'd sat cross-legged in rows on the highly polished but chilly floor. Had it been excitement at seeing their friends after the Christmas holidays that caused some to lay an arm companionably around their neighbour's waist or shoulders, or had they just been seeking a further source of warmth besides the pashminas they were allowed to wear over their uniforms during cold snaps? Their brightly coloured wraps had reminded me of my mum and dad's Christmas tin of Quality Street.

Oriana sighed. 'My first choice would be Monopoly – it's so good for practising number bonds and percentages.'

'Huh! It will only teach the girls the divisiveness of being rich and greedy at the expense of others,' huffed Mavis.

Oriana wasn't fazed by Mavis's outburst.

'You're as bad as Hairnet,' she said. 'She hates Monopoly because it doesn't give players the opportunity to assist others. She told me once she'd like there to be at least one square to provide the opportunity to donate to charity or support the poor.'

I considered for a moment. 'But it would be good for teaching basic business principles.'

Felicity Button, who was jotting down our names and choices in a small notebook, looked up. She was in charge of the programme for essential life skills. 'Don't worry,' she said, 'we've got business principles on the curriculum for next term.'

'So please put me down for cribbage instead, Felicity,' Oriana continued. 'I like playing cards, and cribbage is a painless way of practising mental arithmetic, and a bit more intellectually stimulating than Happy Families, which Hairnet's nabbed for herself.'

'Pictionary for me, please,' said Hazel Taylor, head of art, rubbing her hands together in enthusiasm.

'I'll take Operation!' cried Dr Fleming, head of science, and everybody laughed.

Nicolette Renoir, head of French, frowned for a moment, then brightened. 'Ah, we called it *Docteur Maboule* in France. In French, that means Doctor Crazy Person!'

Even Mavis laughed at that.

'Good thing the girls have already learned first aid in a previous life skills project,' said Judith Gosling, head of history, 'or else we'd be in trouble. I'll take chess, if nobody else wants it. I like a challenge.'

Then she looked at me, her head on one side. 'Miss Lamb, knowing how much you like solving mysteries, do I take it you'll go for Cluedo?'

I grinned at her reference to my role the previous term in exposing an unscrupulous fraudster whose antics had nearly shut St Bride's down.

'Oh please, no more sleuthing, Gemma!' cried Mavis. 'I was hoping for a less eventful term this time around.'

'Me too, Mavis,' I said with feeling. 'Anyway, as we left the staff meeting Joe called first dibs on Cluedo.'

Nicolette's face lit up again. 'Ah, Cluedo! We have the Cluedo too in France, but our pieces have different names. *Par exemple, Madamoiselle Rose avec le poignard dans la salle á manger!*'

I smiled. 'That's the one. I'll take Scrabble, please, if no one else wants it? I used to play Scrabble with my parents all the time when I was a child.'

We'd resumed this comforting habit over the Christmas holidays.

Felicity looked up from her notebook again. 'Did you hear Hairnet's asked Max to join in? She's offered him the choice of poker or roulette.'

Max's full moniker was Max Security – the security guard for the school.

'*Les jeux sont faits! Rien ne va plus!*' said Nicolette lightly.

I smiled, recognising the jargon of the roulette table in phrases I'd learned in French lessons when I was a schoolgirl. Mavis was looking at Nicolette blankly, so she translated.

'You say in English: the bets are made. The die is cast. Hairnet has made her decision. It does not matter whether Max wants or does not want to play the games. Like the girls, he must do as he is told.'

'He ought to feel flattered to be allowed to teach the girls for a change,' I suggested. 'It's a compliment that Hairnet trusts him so much. So, Nicolette, are you going to have to fight Max for roulette?'

A gentle smile softened the strong lines of her features.

'No,' she said. 'I do not like the gambling. I will play Uno with the girls. The name is the same in English, I think. It is the game of cards I used to play with my *grandmère*. She taught me to play and we had happy times together. I think of her each time I play. I miss her still. I think she would approve of Hairnet's plan.'

'The old games are the best,' said Mavis, returning to Old Faithful for a refill. 'I'll do Consequences. I confess I'm glad you didn't beat me to it, Gemma. I'd have thought it was the obvious choice for an English teacher.'

I groaned. 'That would be too much like teaching an English lesson. I want to have fun on our Saturday afternoon games sessions.'

'Consequences?' Nicolette creased her brow. 'What are these consequences?'

Mavis and I exchanged knowing looks, and she nodded at me to explain.

'Consequences is the name of a traditional party game. Great for sleepovers too. Each player has a strip of paper and a pencil, and they write down the component parts of a story in turn, running down the page. They each start with a boy's name, then a girl's name, and where they met. Then they put what he said, what she said, what the consequence was and what the world said. After they've written each answer, they fold the top of the paper to hide their entry and pass it to their neighbour, who writes the next item, and so on. Then, when they're all done, they pass the papers on again, open them up and read the resulting stories aloud. It's great fun. Sometimes the results are hysterical.'

Mavis meanwhile had moved onto the practicalities.

'Scrap paper,' she said abruptly. 'If I'm to teach Consequences I'll need plenty of scrap paper. There'll be none in the library's recycling box so early in the term, and I'll be damned if I'm tearing up fresh paper for such a frivolous exercise. Either of you got a secret stash in your classrooms that I can nab?'

Before we could reply, the staffroom door creaked open and we all turned to see who the new arrival was. Joe Spryke, head of PE, sauntered in with the day's morning post.

After flashing me a smile that warmed me more than any pashmina could, he began to sort the post into the wooden rack of staff pigeonholes that hung on the wall by the door.

As he dropped each letter with a familiar *thunk* into the appropriate slot, he called over his shoulder, 'So what did you make of Hairnet's challenge to the girls in assembly just now, ladies?'

Mavis tutted. 'That guff about New Year resolutions?'

Unruffled by Mavis's harsh tone, Nicolette corrected her. 'It was not about the usual resolutions but about "creative intentions"...'

Hairnet's carefully considered speech had provided a fresh approach to the start of the new year. She counselled the girls to list not what they should give up, but instead to plan new positive activities.

'New Year resolutions assume your starting point is as a flawed human being,' she had explained. 'I know and you know that you are all quite delightful. But there is always room for a little improvement with some positive thinking. Instead of pledging to forego sweets, for example, you might make room in your day to eat an apple.'

Although St Bride's sometimes felt like a fantasy world of Hairnet's making, underneath she was a pragmatist. I was quick to defend her to Mavis now.

'I think she made perfect sense. It's much more achievable to get a hundred children to eat fruit than to stop them eating sweets.'

Mavis pressed her lips together in a hard, straight line before she spoke.

'Less damaging to tuck shop revenue too,' she added.

To demonstrate my support for Hairnet's approval, I turned to a fresh page in my planner, picked up my pen, and wrote 'creative intentions' in block capitals across the top. Unsure what to write next, I glanced up at Nicolette, then Joe.

'So have either of you set your creative intentions yet?'

After depositing the last piece of post, Joe picked up a memo block from the table in front of the pigeonholes and tore off the top sheet. He sauntered over to join us.

'If you lend me your pen, Gemma, I'll write mine down right now. I have only one.'

As he scribbled on the yellow square, he shielded it carefully from our view. With a self-satisfied smile, he returned my pen and made a show of folding the note several times, as if demonstrating the ancient art of origami. Then he sealed it with a tiny length of sticky tape from the dispenser on the table.

'There, that's mine done. Two words is all I need.'

Mavis stirred her coffee more than it required, slopping a little into the saucer. 'Let me guess. Grow up? Keep quiet? For an athlete, you set a very low bar.'

Joe knew and liked Mavis well enough not to take offence.

'I'll tell you on the last day before half term,' he said, 'on Valentine's Day. I'm quietly confident of success.'

On impulse, I reached out, eager to know whether Joe's intention involved me, but he held the little yellow note above his head.

'You'll have to wait and see, Gemma.' He strolled across to Old Faithful. 'In the meantime, this declaration of intent is going to live here at the back of my pigeonhole. Paws off, everyone, until the Day of Reckoning.'

As he helped himself to coffee, I stared at the blank page of my planner, wondering what his two words could be. I suspected I'd need rather more to express my own creative intentions.

A rustling sound distracted me from my thoughts as Nicolette extracted the centre pages of the local paper and, holding them aloft, found herself peering at Mavis through a neatly scissored rectangular hole in the business section.

'You'd make a terrible spy, Nicolette,' remarked Mavis. 'Honestly, you'd think Hairnet would have better things to do with her time than censoring the local paper.'

Curious, she heaved herself up from her chair to go peer, frowning, over Nicolette's shoulder at the mysterious hole.

'It's such an awful rag,' sighed Oriana, who had draped herself languidly on the window seat. 'I wonder anyone buys it at all. Weekly papers are so last century. Their so-called news is obsolete by the time each edition hits the newsagents' shelves. I can find all the news I need online, up to the minute and for free, thank you very much. I don't want to waste my time on trivial nonsense like lost dogs. I mean, who cares?'

Mavis folded her arms across her chest. 'Don't be so flippant, Oriana. You know very well the last time she did this was to cover up a scandal that nearly closed the school.'

Oriana looked quickly away.

'It's probably a complete non-story this time that she just doesn't want to trouble us about, especially so early in the term when we're all fresh back from the Christmas holidays.'

Joe took a sip of his coffee. 'My money's on the MP with the daughter in Year 9.'

Nicolette raised her eyebrows. 'For a matter of finance, or an *affaire du cœur*?'

Mavis perked up.

'Hmm, a juicy romantic rumour in the run-up to Valentine's Day would be a gift to bored reporters,' she mused.

Nicolette replaced the centre spread, closed and folded the newspaper, and returned it to the coffee table, ready for the next reader.

I turned to Joe. 'Does Hairnet really censor the staffroom copy of the local paper? She strikes me as being more in favour of free speech than censorship.'

'Yes, up to a point. But when it comes to protecting the school, she'll do whatever it takes. End of story.'

When Joe coughed, I realised that all this talk of intrusive reporters must have been making him uncomfortable. Until now the school had managed to conceal from the local paper that there was a discredited national athlete hiding in its midst, disguised as a female PE teacher, but if they ever found out, it would be all over their front page in no time. Once the nationals picked it up too, the school's credibility as a safe haven for adolescent girls would be shattered.

Meanwhile, Oriana had been called to the staffroom door at the request of one of the younger girls. After she had dismissed her and closed the door, she strolled across to stand beside Joe before addressing me.

'Gemma, darling, could you do me a favour and mop up little Veronica Thyssen? Imogen's just told me she's bawling on her bed, and I haven't time to deal with her now.'

As Oriana's deputy in the Poorhouse – like all the houses, ours was named after a saint, Clare, in our case, founder of the Order of the Poor Clares, hence the girls' jocular nickname for it – I had no choice but to comply, but I couldn't help feeling disgruntled. Oriana had a free period first thing, whereas I was timetabled to teach Year 7. As soon as the bell rang for the start of morning lessons, I closed my planner and slipped my pen into my pencil case.

'Any clues as to what's upsetting her?'

'Clues? Ha, ever the sleuth. Well, I don't suppose she's homesick so early in the term. And she's not usually the demonstrative type.' Unlike some of her peers, I thought, who would speak their minds and show their emotions without the slightest inhibition.

'She doesn't seem the spoiled type, either,' I added. 'Whenever she gets one of those Harrods parcels her father sends her every week, she's nothing but generous. She shares the contents with her friends, barely keeping a thing for herself.'

Oriana raised a forefinger. 'Ah, I remember now. She was mumbling some nonsense about afternoon tea. Don't worry, Gemma, you'll snap her out of it in no time, whatever it is. Now, Joe, I need to borrow you for a moment. Come with me.'

Without more ado, she herded Joe into the furthest corner of the staffroom for privacy. By the time I reached the door, she had backed him against the wall and begun to talk to him in an urgent voice, too low for me to grasp a word of what she was saying.

2

FOR THE LOVE OF DOILIES

It seemed I'd have to put investigating the mystery of the missing newspaper article on hold until after I'd dealt with Veronica's crisis, but I was determined to return to it at the first opportunity.

As I strode up the great marble stairs, the staff-only route to the dormitories, I tried to remember whether Veronica had experienced any upsets the previous term. I didn't know of any friendship issues. In fact, all the other girls wanted to keep in with her to share the spoils from her Harrods parcels. I was glad Veronica didn't appear to have noticed their motivation. Nor was schoolwork a problem. She always submitted her prep on time, and her work was neat and competent.

On her report card at the end of the previous term, my only criticism of her progress had been that she needed to make more effort to join in the conversation in the classroom. Several other teachers had said the same, and Hairnet had called a staff meeting to discuss her situation. Just why was she so quiet, when she was clearly a clever and capable learner? We concluded that being so tall for her age put her at a social disadvantage. She was just entering the gawky stage. Towering over most of her teachers as well as her peer group would make her even more self-conscious than the average adolescent. Perhaps she was reluctant to draw any further attention to herself by speaking up in class.

When I entered the Poorhouse Year 7 dormitory, several of Veronica's classmates were clustered about her bed, where she lay flat out, face down, shoulders heaving with silent sobs. I was glad to see her friends were supportive even when she had no Harrods treats to dispense, but their attempts to comfort her seemed to be having little effect.

'There's always next term,' Imogen was saying, stroking Veronica's limp hand. 'I mean, next half-term. We're all going to go to Doilies again when we come back from our half-term holiday.'

Poppy, cross-legged at the foot of the bed, was hugging Veronica's pyjama case, a froth of artificial fur in the shape of a sleeping sloth. The pyjama case had been the one item Veronica had kept for herself from her last Harrods box.

'Just ask your dad to put it in his diary now,' said Poppy. 'Then he can keep that day free and he won't have to dash off, like he did last time.'

Kneeling beside Poppy was Simone. 'You won't regret it, Vee. Their chocolate cake is absolutely to die for. You'll love it.'

As I approached the bed, Imogen leaned closer to Veronica.

'Look, Miss Lamb's come to see you,' she said. 'She cares about you too.'

As the girls scattered to make way for me to sit on the bed beside their weeping friend, I laid a comforting hand gently on her shoulder.

'Hello, Veronica, I'm sorry you're so sad. Why don't you sit up and tell me all about it? Maybe I'll be able to do something to make it better.'

I hoped so, although at this stage I wasn't sure what.

Veronica took a deep, snuffling breath, before raising herself up on her elbows to gaze at me. Her eyes were as pink as a rabbit's, her cheeks as wet as an eel's.

'I don't think you can, Miss. I don't think anyone can.'

Hopping from one foot to the other beside the bed, Imogen put her hand up for permission to speak.

'We've tried really hard, Miss, honest. We invited Veronica and her dad to join us at Doilies for tea next time we go. We really want them to come.'

I surveyed the earnest faces of Veronica's assembled friends before I replied. A couple of them were tear-stained in empathy.

'I'm sure you've all been very kind. But the bell will be going any minute now, so run along, girls, and get ready for your first lesson. You're with me for English, and I don't want any of you to be late. Not you, Veronica.' I laid my hand on her shoulder to stay her, as she was about to swing her legs over the side of the bed. 'Let's you and I have a little chat first and see what we can do to make you feel better.'

As we waited for her friends to leave the dormitory, Veronica shuffled backwards into a sitting position, leaning her back against the battered oak headboard. Over the years it must have propped up dozens of girls as they passed through the school and out into the world.

'There really isn't anything to be done now, Miss. I've missed my chance.'

'Why? Doilies hasn't closed down, has it?'

'No, what I mean is, I've missed my chance for the tea party my friends were having at the start of term. At the end of the Christmas term, we all agreed that on the day we came back to school, we'd meet for afternoon tea at Doilies, the tea room in the Excelsior Hotel in Cirencester. We didn't have to be in school until five o'clock, so we had plenty of time for tea.'

For want of something helpful to do, I smoothed her crumpled duvet cover, recognising from its distinctive pattern the signature work of an expensive designer.

'So what happened to stop you? Did you and your dad get stuck in traffic on the drive down from London? Did that flurry of snow slow you down? It can be a slow and dreary drive down the motorway at this time of year.'

I reached for the sloth at the foot of her bed and fluffed it up a little before handing it to her. Hugging the sloth to her chest, Veronica frowned.

'We were a bit late leaving London because Daddy had to finish a phone call. He's always making phone calls. My nanny never minds phoning her family in Poland on our landline because she says he won't notice because our telephone bill must be huge.'

That her father kept a nanny on after Veronica had started boarding school showed how little time he had for her in the holidays. The poor child had lost her mother to cancer at a young age, and her nanny must have been the closest she had to a second parent at home.

'But Daddy said if he put his foot on it, we'd still get to Doilies in time for at least part of the party. Then he got another phone call when we were leaving the motorway to say they wanted him urgently back at the office, so he said we wouldn't have time to stop at Cirencester. He'd only have time to drop me at school and shoot straight back up to London.'

I remembered exchanging a few words with Mr Thyssen in the entrance hall as he'd brought in Veronica's trunk the previous afternoon, and he'd given me the impression that he couldn't get away fast enough. He seemed a man of few words. Their home life must be near-silent. I hoped the nanny was the chatty, companionable kind.

Veronica sniffled, and I passed her a fresh tissue from the red velvet box on her bedside table.

'So Daddy dropped me and my stuff at school and left. He didn't even stop to say hello to Miss Bliss or Miss Harnett.'

Members of staff were always on duty in the entrance hall to welcome the girls back – and to butter up the parents.

'It can't have been much fun for your father either, having to drive straight back to work without so much as a cup of tea to keep him going.'

'That's just what I thought. It was another reason we should have had tea and cake at the Excelsior. It would have given him a rest.' She sighed and blew her nose. 'And I did so want to see what Doilies was like for myself. All my friends have been there, and I never have.'

When the bell rang for the start of the first lesson, Veronica set the sloth neatly on her pillow, jumped off the bed, and stretched her arms above her head. She'd grown even taller during the holidays.

Once she'd grabbed her pashmina and we'd both picked up our book bags, we headed for the courtyard, where she was due to join me in my classroom.

'Why don't you do as Imogen said and message your dad tonight after prep? You can ask him to keep the first day of next term free to take you to Doilies. He'll probably be more in the mood for some nice tea and cake then. I dare say he was still full of the lovely Christmas cake you made and took home for him.'

Veronica held the classroom door open for me.

'Maybe, but I'm not holding my breath. He'll only have another excuse, even if it's not work. I bet he'll tell me he's given up cake for Lent.'

She pulled her pashmina more tightly around her shoulders and headed for her usual desk at the back of the classroom.

3

BREAD AND BUTTER LETTERS

This morning I was due to teach my Year 7 class about the etiquette of formal letter-writing, a topic we'd begun the previous term, as dictated by the lesson plans left for me by my predecessor, Katie Donovan. Grateful as I was for these guidelines, I wondered whether Katie's misdemeanours, which I'd learned about the previous term, had been the subject of earlier episodes of Hairnet's censorship. But that little scandal was long past. I couldn't begin to imagine what the new rumours might be. But then the bell rang, and I had no choice but to focus on my lesson.

Today I decided to add a seasonal touch by focusing on Christmas thank you letters. I opened the lesson with a question.

'How many of you have written thank-you letters to people who gave you Christmas presents?'

For a moment, the girls looked at each other, trying to anticipate their friends' replies before responding. Then Poppy's hand shot up.

'My grandma calls them bread-and-butter letters.'

'Why, does she eat them in sandwiches?' some wit piped up. The rest of the class giggled.

In my first term at St Bride's, I'd realised good teachers must develop the timing of stand-up comedians, riding any laughter and using it to their advantage before delivering their next line. I allowed the laughter to die down before I spoke again.

'There's a good reason your grandma calls them that. It's the term used in the olden days when people were invited to stay in country houses. For those on a low income, being a house guest could save them a lot of money. Thank-you letters were thus an indirect way of earning their keep, not just bread and butter, but meals and entertainment and heating and lighting, not to mention the opportunities to meet important, influential people. They weren't just being polite when they wrote to their hosts. They were also increasing the chance of being invited back.'

When I paused to allow the girls to digest this information, Imogen's hand shot up, wiggling her fingers in her eagerness to comment.

'Yes, Imogen?'

'So if we write thank you letters for Christmas presents, does that mean we'll be more likely to get more presents from those people in future?'

I bit back a smile. 'What do you think? Would you be more inclined to send presents to someone who thanked you nicely?'

There were murmurs of assent.

'Now back to my official question. Which of you has already sent all your Christmas thank-you letters?'

Veronica's and Christabel's hands shot up straight away, and a couple of other girls' wavered halfway, to show they'd started but not finished.

'Does it count if I write just one letter and send it to Father Christmas?' asked Julia brightly. She was a slight child with white-blonde hair who could have passed for about eight years old.

I wondered whether the cheeky twinkle in her eye meant she was joking. These girls, with their sheltered lives, seemed to take longer to grow up than most, and I didn't want to give her an untimely awakening about Santa if she truly still believed in him. Poppy came to my rescue.

'No, silly, Santa's just the delivery driver. Like a white-van man, only with longer working hours and more environmentally friendly because of his reindeer.'

Everyone laughed.

I turned to Christabel, still patiently holding up her hand.

'Do we have to write to everyone who gave us presents, Miss?' asked Christabel. 'I've written to all the people I know in person, but what about my godmother in Austria who I haven't seen since my christening? Does she count?'

'Is she your fairy godmother, like in *Sleeping Beauty*?' asked Julia. 'Hers only went to her christening too.'

Wondering whether Julia was trying to wind me up, I moved the conversation swiftly along.

'What do you think, girls? How would you feel if you were Christabel's godmother and had sent her a lovely gift and didn't receive a thank-you letter?'

'Cross.'

'Offended.'

'Sad.'

'Miffed.'

Christabel held up her hand. 'Okay, I'll write to her now.'

I picked up a pile of plain, mauve notepaper from my desk and handed it to the nearest girl with instructions to distribute a few sheets to each pupil.

'So, first exercise for the day, girls: in your planner, make a list of all the people you still have to write thank-you letters to. When you've finished your list, start writing your first letter on this pretty stationery.'

Soon all but Veronica and Christabel were bent over their desks scribbling lists of names and presents.

'What about us?' asked Christabel. 'What should we do?'

'You can write letters to any of your family members who you think might like to receive a cheery New Year greeting from you. Grandmas? Grandpas? Aunties? Neighbours?'

The two girls looked at each other for a moment before starting to write.

For the next few minutes, I strolled up and down the aisles between the girls' desks, glancing at their work to make sure they were on the right track. I was pleased to see they had remembered the previous term's lesson about the correct layout of a traditional letter.

I paused at Veronica's side on the pretext of checking her spelling, but really to gauge whether she was feeling more cheerful now. I couldn't tell from her expression or body language, and hoped she wasn't just putting on a brave face while still crying inside.

Dear Sharon,

Her letter began.

'Who's Sharon?' I asked, hoping to make conversation. 'Is she a relative or a friend?'

Veronica carried on writing without looking up. 'Sharon's Daddy's new PA. She's doing all Daddy's present shopping now. She's much better than the old one.'

But if it's with Daddy's money, I was about to say, shouldn't you be thanking Daddy? Then I reconsidered. Why shouldn't she thank Sharon for her thoughtfulness? I wondered whether Veronica's father ever gave his PA due praise.

They all scribbled away happily until I clapped my hands for their attention towards the end of the lesson.

'Okay, pens down, please, girls. You can finish your thank-you letters as this evening's prep, and, if you need to, you can also use your free time.'

A few girls groaned.

'No complaining, please, girls. Needing to thank a multitude of people for presents is a good problem to have.'

The groaners gave apologetic smiles.

'Now, next lesson we will be writing a different kind of letter. I'll tell you a little about it now, so that you can be thinking about it in the meantime. Do you remember what Miss Harnett was saying in assembly this morning about setting your intentions for the new term? Well, tomorrow, we're going to write letters listing our creative intentions for this term. They will be addressed to a very important person. Who do you think that will be?'

'Miss Harnett?'

'To each other?'

'To you, Miss?'

'You're not going to put them on social media, are you, Miss?'

There was a collective gasp at this suggestion.

'Miss, I don't want anyone else reading my letter.'

I held up a hand for silence.

'Don't worry, the only person to read your letter will be you – unless you want to share it with anyone else. Not even I will see it. I won't be marking it. You are to address it to yourself, writing down your intentions for between now and half-term. Keep your letter somewhere safe and reread it as often as you like for inspiration. Then in our last English lesson before half-term, we will all bring our letters to class and read them again to see to what extent we have fulfilled our intentions. But tonight, please concentrate on finishing your thank-you letters. We'll talk more about creative intentions in tomorrow's lesson.'

Poppy put up her hand.

'Are you going to write a letter to yourself too, Miss,' she said, 'and fulfil your creative intentions?'

I pictured the blank page of my daybook where I'd been struggling to define them that morning.

'Of course.' I sounded more confident than I felt.

4

CHANGE AFOOT

The first few days of term passed in a flurry of activity as I re-adjusted to the rigid school timetable, where all our waking hours were dictated by the school bell. I was looking forward to escaping from the campus for an afternoon coffee date with Joe. I also planned a little detour to the Wendlebury Barrow village shop to buy an intact local paper. I wanted to find out what it was that Hairnet didn't want us to see, before it disappeared off the shelves to make way for the next week's edition, and to discuss the matter in confidence with Joe.

Then my plans were scuppered once more by Oriana.

'Gemma, would you please do me an enormous favour?'

As her deputy, I could hardly say no to her request.

'No problem, Oriana. What is it, and when?'

She took my empty coffee cup to return to the staffroom trolley.

'Oh, I just need you to stay in school this afternoon while I pop out to attend to some personal business.'

'Today? But Wednesday is my afternoon off.'

She gazed at me, all wide-eyed innocence, although she was well aware of my timetable.

'I'm sorry it's such short notice, Gemma, but you know how it is sometimes.'

I had no idea what she meant by 'how it is', but her evasive tone deterred me from asking any questions in the middle of the busy staffroom. I assumed it must be urgent for her to miss teaching a class. Perhaps she needed to go into town for medical reasons. I didn't want to make her feel awkward by asking her what it was in case it was something embarrassing. I hoped it was nothing serious.

She took my silence as consent.

'Anyway,' she continued, 'you don't need to actually teach any of my lessons. Just sit in my classroom while the girls do work I've prepared for them.'

So, she'd be missing more than one lesson.

I glanced at Joe. I was surprised to see him reading the fashion pages of *The Times* in his favourite armchair, with such studied concentration that I suspected he was listening to our every word.

'Gemma,' Oriana began again, 'you didn't have plans to go out yourself, did you?'

When her voice quavered, I realised how important this outing must be for her.

Joe looked up from his paper and shook his head to release me from our date: a cream tea at Hector's House, a bookshop-cum-café in Wendlebury Barrow. Wednesday afternoon was the only time that we were both free that week, so Oriana's request meant postponing our date for seven days.

I forced a smile. 'No, that's fine.'

Oriana released her breath.

'Thanks, Gemma, I owe you. I've left worksheets for each lesson on my desk in my classroom. All you need do is hand them out and supervise quiet working. The Year 11 and 12 classes shouldn't need any help, they're just revising, but if any of the Year 7 girls need reminding of how to multiply and divide fractions, ask Veronica to demonstrate on the board. She can do the sums as well as I can and with more enthusiasm. I'm hoping her attitude might rub off on the less eager girls.'

Oriana ran her hands over her neatly bobbed hair, which, unusually, was currently its natural colour. Scarcely a week went by when she didn't give herself a makeover, and I wondered how the girls' fathers recognised her from one Parents' Evening to the next.

She was about to dash out of the staffroom door when I called her back.

'While you're out, Oriana, could you please do me a favour too and pick up a copy of the local paper?'

She scowled at me.

'Whatever do you want that rag for?' she replied.

'Oh, just for a project with the Year 9s,' I improvised.

She gave a heavy sigh. 'I'll try to remember.'

As the door closed behind her, Joe lowered his newspaper.

'That was very good of you, Gemma.'

I shrugged. 'Yes, it was. I don't mind doing her the odd favour, especially if she does one for me sometimes, but I'm still disappointed by her thoughtless timing. You know I'd rather spend the afternoon out with you.'

Joe folded the paper, dropped it on to the coffee table, and rose from his chair.

'Never mind. There'll be another Wednesday next week I promise. Shall we say same time, same place?'

I sighed. 'Yes, please. Thanks, Joe.'

As he passed me on his way to the door, his arm brushed mine, making my spine tingle.

In the context of a school term, a week was an awfully long time.

* * *

As Oriana predicted, the first two lessons of the afternoon were easy to supervise, giving me time to catch up with my marking while the girls completed Oriana's worksheets. I was glad of Veronica's presence in the Year 7 lesson as she demonstrated to the rest of the class, with admirable precision and logic, how to solve the first of the sums set in their worksheet. I recalled that her English prep was always the neatest in my class. Her love of order and reasoning would take her a long way in life beyond school.

While they were working, and once I was up to date with marking, I decided to write a letter to my parents. I'd emailed and texted them since my return to St Bride's, but talking to the Year 7s in our lesson earlier in the week had reminded me how much nicer it was to receive a physical letter in the handwriting of someone you love, rather than in the anonymous digital font of electronic messages. From my bookbag I pulled out a sheet of school notepaper that I'd taken from the staffroom stationery cupboard. The thick cream paper bore the school's crest: a shield featuring the green rush cross, one of the symbols of St Bride, against a white background. The slightly wonky appearance of the cross seemed an appropriate emblem for this quirky school.

I laid down my red marking pen and scrabbled in my pencil case for my blue one, before remembering that I'd lent it to Mavis in the staffroom at lunchtime, when she was writing a new sign for the library noticeboard. Mavis didn't use computers unless she absolutely had to. Assuming that, like most teachers, Oriana would keep a supply of spare pens in her desk, I wrenched open the top drawer and pulled out at random a sugar-pink ballpoint. Gold letters along the barrel advertised a local cosmetic surgery service in Cirencester. Rolling it between my fingers, I discovered a second legend on the opposite side: 'Discretion guaranteed.'

If Hairnet saw this pen in school, she'd have a fit. She didn't want the girls to worry about their appearance or body image. While her school rules required them to be well-groomed in their neat uniforms, which she considered good training for the world of work, vanity was actively discouraged. Make-up and hair dye were banned, and hairstyles any more elaborate than a functional ponytail or plait were frowned upon.

No wonder Oriana had kept the pen out of sight. I threw it to the back of the drawer and pulled out a plain blue ballpoint instead.

Dear Mum and Dad,
   I hope you're both well

I wrote, but I was still thinking about Oriana.
Perhaps Oriana was entirely well too, and her appointment this after-

noon was not with her GP for a worrying illness, or to the dentist for an urgent problem with a tooth, but to this plastic surgeon for a cosmetic procedure. Now her elusiveness about the purpose of her trip began to make sense. If there had been something medically wrong with her, she was not the type to keep quiet about it. Feeling the need for cosmetic surgery was quite a different matter. She'd hardly announce in the staffroom, 'I'm feeling a bit ugly today, so can you cover my lesson while I have an urgent bit of cosmetic surgery?'

I chewed on the end of Oriana's pen. So much for my supposed sleuthing skills. It was absurd of me to reach such a dramatic conclusion on such flimsy evidence. Not even Oriana would bunk off school for Botox. Possessing this pen no more made her a candidate for cosmetic surgery than the pencil in my pencil case advertising one of the girl's father's wealth management service made me a billionaire. It was just a free pen. There must be an innocent explanation. But it was unlike Oriana not to speak her mind if something was troubling her.

By the time the bell rang at the end of the lesson, I was wishing I'd pressed Oriana to tell me the true purpose of her trip to Cirencester, to quash another assumption that I was trying to suppress: that this term she had decided to hit on Joe.

5

CAUGHT OUT

As I strolled back from the classroom courtyard to the main school building, I began to realise why so far this term Oriana had kept her natural look, instead of going through the succession of changes I'd witnessed the previous term. Joe wouldn't be fooled or impressed by yet another makeover. He'd known her too long and too well to be interested in anything other than her true self.

As I approached the entrance hall, I heard the distinctive thud of the front door closing. A rush of cold air chilled my ankles, and the familiar tip-tap of high heels on the marble floor told me that Oriana had returned. I tried to sound casual.

'Hi, Oriana. Did you have a successful mission?'

She gave a stiff smile. Stiff enough to indicate Botox? Or just the aftermath of a dental anaesthetic? Her brisk reply gave nothing away.

'All fine, thank you, Gemma.'

She put her hand on the bannisters, ready to head up the stairs.

'And did you get my newspaper?' I asked.

She clapped a hand to her forehead. 'Sorry, Gemma, I completely forgot.'

She flashed a smile so phoney that I was convinced she was lying.

'Anyway,' she said, 'I'll just drop my coat at my flat before supper. See you later.'

She nodded towards the Trough, as if willing me to head there now and leave her alone.

I had a sudden inkling that she knew what the missing article contained. What secrets did she want kept?

As the bell hadn't yet rung for supper, I lingered in the hall and watched her glide away from me up the curving stairs.

To kill time, I decided to do the bursar a favour by bolting the front door for the night. It was turning into my day for doing people favours.

As I was about to shoot the thick brass bolt across, the door handle rattled, making me leap back in surprise. It was a bit late for visitors, so as I opened the door, I held the knob firmly in case I needed to bar an unwanted intruder. Even though Max patrolled with such impressive vigilance he was practically omnipresent, the estate was so huge that you could never be too careful, especially after dark. I was glad of the hubbub of girls now swarming down from their dorms towards the Trough, so it would be clear to any visitor that I wasn't alone.

The caller's grip was stronger than mine, and as he swung open the door he nearly knocked me off my feet.

'Ooh, hello, Gemma, what are you doing here?'

Muffled in an androgynous waxed jacket, jeans, and walking boots, Joe gave me a cheerful smile. I frowned back at him.

'More to the point, what are you doing outside at this hour? Are you coming back from the sports field? I thought you had no lessons this afternoon.'

When he shook his head, I couldn't help but conclude that he'd been waiting outside for a few moments. Perhaps he'd just come back from Cirencester with Oriana and wanted to hide the fact they'd been out together for the afternoon.

He stepped over the threshold, closed the door behind him and fastened the bolt.

I tried again. 'Surely you haven't been out cycling in those heavy boots?'

'Actually, I accepted a lift into Cirencester with Oriana. I needed to buy some new parts for one of my bikes.' So I'd been right. 'I've just dropped them off at the bike shed, ready to install it tomorrow.'

It was true there was a shop in Cirencester that sold bicycle parts, and to take advantage of Oriana's car rather than cycle there in this cold, damp weather, on road slippery with thawing snow, made perfect sense. So why did I feel so uneasy about his reply? Suddenly, a more shocking explanation dawned on me. It wasn't Oriana seeking cosmetic surgery, but Joe, in an attempt to shake off his scandal-ridden past once and for all, and to keep him safe from detection from the press beyond the sanctuary of St Bride's.

Joe glanced over my shoulder towards the Trough. 'So, has the supper bell gone yet? I'm starving.'

Realising he wasn't going to tell me any more about their outing, and with a heavy heart, I headed at his side for the Trough.

6

PHOTOGRAPHIC EVIDENCE

'Miss Lamb, Miss Lamb!'

The Year 7 girls on my dining table seemed desperate to tell me their exciting news.

As I took my seat at the head of their table, I surveyed their eager faces, all but one of which was turned towards me. Only Veronica, seated on my right, was gazing at her empty plate.

'First things first, girls. Please help each other to supper and then you can share your news.'

As soon as a slice of lasagne and a pile of curly green salad lay on every plate, the girls began to explain. One at a time, going around the table, each added a point of detail, reminding me of Mavis's Consequences.

'You know you were saying in our English lesson about writing letters to ourselves?'

'About what we should try to change by half-term.'

'How to be our best selves.'

'How to live our best lives.'

'Well, we thought we'd like to do something else to add context.'

I smiled. 'Well done, Angelica, good use of vocabulary.'

Angelica beamed as she turned to hear the next girl speak.

'We thought it might help if we also reminded ourselves about how we used to be.'

'So should all take photos of ourselves now, at the start of term, to see if we look any different.'

I considered for a moment. 'That's an interesting idea, although I'm not sure we'd see a big physical change in just a few weeks.'

Imogen held up her hand.

'I know!' she said. 'Let's get our dads to send us our baby pictures. Then we can see how much we've changed in our whole lives.'

Poppy spread her hands above the table mimicking a conjuror's flourish.

'We'll see ourselves transformed at a glance! Shazam! Abracadabra!'

'We've got heaps of baby pictures of me at home,' said Imogen. 'I'm sure my dad can spare one.'

'And me.'

'And me.'

Louisa sighed and rolled her eyes. 'There are studio photos of me all over the walls in my house. It's so embarrassing.'

I smiled at their bright faces, made warm and rosy by the steam rising from their plates of lasagne.

'That's a lovely idea, girls. A very interesting addition to the project. Well done, everyone, for using your imagination to add value to your work.'

Imogen put her hand up. 'Would the teachers like to join in? Can you ask your dad to send us a baby photo of you?'

I thought of the snap of me cuddling my toy bunny that had stood on my parents' piano for as long as I could remember. The girls would find it highly amusing.

Poppy raised her hand. 'Maybe we could run a competition, Miss? We could display all the photos in the library and people would have to guess who was who.'

I considered for a moment.

'Photos of all one hundred girls, plus the staff too?' I mused aloud. 'That would keep everyone puzzling until half-term.' Given the gloomy weather and long dark evenings, that might have been no bad thing, and

Hairnet liked to encourage initiative. 'Why don't a couple of you go to see Miss Harnett after supper to suggest it? But first check with Miss Brook whether she'd allow you to take up so much space in the library. Now, let's get on with our supper before your lovely lasagne gets cold.'

Amid a hum of enthusiastic chatter, with the girls describing their favourite baby photos of themselves to any of their friends who would listen, they began to tuck in. Only Veronica remained silent, eating tiny mouthfuls very slowly.

I leaned towards her to speak in a low voice.

'Are you okay, Veronica?'

She didn't look up from her plate.

'I'm all right, Miss. It's just that I don't know whether Daddy's got any baby photos of me. He put all our family photos away after Mummy died. He said I reminded him too much of her. Sometimes I think he just doesn't want to look at me in real life either.'

Two big tears dropped on to her plate.

I gave her arm a little squeeze.

'I very much doubt that. He probably just wants to keep your precious pictures in a safe place so they don't fade.' I thought of the old school photos lining the corridor behind the library. They were so faded that all the staff and pupils seemed to have the same skin tone and hair colour.

'Why did he bother taking them in the first place? Why bother even having me?'

The girl sitting on her other side patted her hand. 'Would you like more lasagne, Veronica?'

Offering seconds to others was the Trough code for wanting second helpings yourself. The girls weren't allowed to take more unless their fellow diners had their fill. To her credit, Veronica turned away from me to sate her neighbour's appetite, leaving me fighting back a tear of sympathy.

7

BEDTIME STORY

'Oh, there you are, Gemma!'

As I returned from the library, where I'd been choosing a new novel after supper, Oriana was standing outside my flat. Having missed my afternoon off, I was looking forward to spending the rest of the evening curled up on my sofa with a good book. I hugged the paperback to my chest.

'Hi, Oriana. Shouldn't you be touring the dorms by now?'

The bell signalling that the youngest girls should be tucked up in bed had already rung. As Oriana wrinkled her nose, I had a sinking feeling that she was about to ask me for another favour.

'Actually, that's why I was trying to find you,' she began. 'I'm expecting an important phone call from Australia, and it should have come by now, but the caller is late and I don't want to miss it. Can you do the night-time rounds?' She shrugged. 'That's the trouble with calls from the other side of the world. There's such a limited window when both parties are awake.'

What's wrong with email? I wanted to say, but I was too tired to argue.

'Okay, okay, just let me put my book in my flat first. I don't think the Year 7s would fancy this as their bedtime story.'

I showed her the front cover of *Orlando* before unlocking the door of my flat. I set Virginia Woolf on my coffee table with a wistful glance at the fireplace, where a pyramid of kindling needed only the touch of a lit match to start a roaring log fire. But before I would allow myself to start reading *Orlando*, I had planned to look up the local paper's website and read the latest issue online. My laptop lay open on the sofa at the ready.

As I marched down the corridor towards the Poorhouse dorms, I heard footsteps in the distance. Their soft tread suggested sports shoes rather than Oriana's high heels. As I turned the corner, I almost bumped into Joe – a welcome surprise that he should come to see me here. My spirits lifted immediately. Perhaps I'd been imagining his preference for Oriana after all. What a shame his visit to me now was so badly timed. I smiled apologetically.

'If you were on your way to see me, I'm afraid I haven't got time right now. Oriana's just delegated tonight's dormitory patrol to me.'

Although the staff weren't allowed in each other's flats, we were permitted to socialise in the corridors outside, which were out of bounds for and out of sight of the girls. There was no rule against staff embracing there. I took a step closer to Joe, but he was already waving me away.

'I thought you'd have been with the girls by now. You'd better leg it. I've just seen Hairnet heading that way. You'll be for it if you're late.'

Only as I was turning the corner did I register that not only was he coming to see Oriana rather than me, but that she must have told him I'd be safely out of their way in the dorms. Was her story of the call from Australia just a ruse to allow her and Joe to spend time alone?

As I arrived at the Year 7 dorm, Hairnet was already standing in the open doorway, looking at her watch. McPhee sat at her feet, casually washing a front paw.

'Sorry I'm late, Miss Harnett, but Oriana only just asked me to cover for her.'

I would not normally rat on Oriana, but I didn't want to get on the wrong side of Hairnet, and, besides, it was true.

Hairnet's expression remained stern as she closed the dormitory door behind her, muffling the girls' cheery chatter as they were settling into bed. I was glad they wouldn't hear her admonish me.

'Now, Miss Lamb, what is this I hear that you're encouraging the girls to solicit baby photos of all the staff?'

So my lateness wasn't the reason for her stern expression.

'Actually, it was the girls' idea, not mine. They suggested it to me at supper tonight as an extension of our letter-to-self project. I was impressed with their creative thinking and I thought you would be too. Comparing and contrasting how our physical looks change over time, as well as what's going on inside, should trigger some interesting discussions.'

Hairnet's shoulders dropped slightly.

'Provided the photos are only of the girls,' she conceded. 'But no staff, please, Miss Lamb. I've already said this to the girls, and now I'm telling you. No staff photos.'

That was a shame. I had been looking forward to seeing my colleagues' baby photos.

'Just be careful, my dear.' I was glad to be her dear again. 'Failing to anticipate the consequences of her actions is what caused your predecessor's downfall.'

Was that a veiled threat? Her words sent a chill right through me and my stomach began to churn.

As Hairnet marched off in the direction of her apartment, McPhee got up, arched his back, and rubbed it companionably against my ankles, before trotting after his mistress.

I entered the dormitory amid a clamour of voices.

'Oh, Miss Lamb, Miss Lamb! Hair – Miss Harnett was just dreadfully cross with us.'

'Why didn't you tell us we're not allowed to ask teachers for their baby photos?'

I went to fetch their storybook of the moment from the shelf.

'I'm sorry, girls, I didn't know until Miss Harnett told me just a second ago. But we all know now, so that's fine. So hush now, and I'll start your bedtime story.'

I opened the ancient hardback of *Swallows and Amazons* at the sky-blue ribbon marker.

As I waited for them all to settle down, I pondered the reason for

Hairnet's ban. Was she worried that displaying baby photos of herself and Oriana would give away their relationship? Did she fear Joe's picture would have people asking questions about his gender?

Poppy announced her theory as she wriggled further down under the covers. 'Maybe Hairnet just doesn't want us to know that she was a very ugly baby.'

The girls giggled.

'Now, now, Poppy, Miss Harnett is a very elegant lady. I'm sure she must have been an equally bonny baby.'

Poppy pulled her duvet up to her chin. 'Okay, but I bet the bursar wasn't.'

Trying not to smile, I began to read.

8

PAPER ROUND

The next morning on waking, and going over the events of the previous day in my head, I felt a little foolish to have wondered whether Oriana or Joe were considering plastic surgery. Not only was Oriana naturally beautiful, she was so adept at transforming her appearance with make-up, hairstyle, and clothing, she needed no other means.

As to Joe, he'd successfully concealed his whereabouts for several years without needing any further form of disguise. He'd already changed his hairstyle beyond recognition. Having previously shaved his head for the sake of aerodynamics, he had allowed his hair to grow unchecked, resulting in long, natural curls.

Even so, as I brushed my hair into a ponytail, to keep it neat during my busy day ahead, I decided I didn't buy Joe's story about their trip to Cirencester. He usually ordered cycle parts online. From the way Oriana had buttonholed him in the staffroom, she seemed intent on taking him with her to Cirencester for her own purposes, but what were they and why did she need him to accompany her? Could something else be afoot between them – interviews at a rival school, for example? No wonder Joe had been so quick to play down the importance of the news stories missing from the local paper. Either that, or they were simply going out on a date.

When Joe and I had spent such a delightful few days together over Christmas, I thought we'd cemented our relationship, even though going back to St Bride's school rules could hamper its progress.

Now it occurred to me that perhaps he hadn't meant our relationship to be exclusive. Was he some kind of commitment-phobe? Or was I just not used to a normal relationship after seven years with the possessive, controlling Steven? Joe had not pledged to be exclusive. I had just assumed we were.

I felt a slight twinge of jealousy at the thought of her enjoying what should have been my afternoon out with Joe. Nor could I forget that it was Oriana who had wangled a job for him at St Bride's in the first place, when he was fresh out of his previous relationship. He might feel obliged now to do whatever she wanted. I wondered whether she'd given herself a sporty makeover in his first term at St Bride's to signal that she was his type.

Mavis had told me Joe and Oriana had only ever been like brother and sister, but if there was nothing between them but platonic friendship, why had Oriana been keen to get me out of the way in order for Joe to visit her last evening? And why had Joe been so stand-offish when he'd bumped into me in the corridor?

After breakfast, I hoped to allay my fears in the staffroom, where all the teachers usually gathered to pick up their post and memos and brace themselves with caffeine for the first lesson of the day. It was a good way to catch up with someone if your paths weren't due to cross until break.

Joe's table in the Trough had finished their breakfast a good ten minutes before my garrulous Year 7s, and by the time I reached the staffroom, he was sitting in his usual armchair, a cup of coffee at his side. He appeared to be engrossed in the local paper, open at the page for jobs and other public notices.

'Not planning on leaving us, are you, Joe?'

I tried to sound jokey, hoping he wouldn't notice my genuine concern.

He closed the paper and looked up to give me a reassuring smile.

'Why, are you trying to get rid of me?'

'No, of course not – it's just that...'

As he gazed at me, I faltered, not wanting to sound possessive or needy.

'Sorry again about yesterday afternoon, Gemma. Let's try again on Sunday afternoon, eh? I know Hector's House doesn't open on Sundays, but we could go somewhere else.'

My spirits lifted.

'I'm happy to drive us somewhere in my car if it's not the weather for a bike ride,' I said.

I'd thought that, to Joe, there was no such thing as unsuitable weather for cycling, but after his lift from Oriana I wasn't so sure. As for myself, I didn't exactly relish biking through muddy lanes in January's wind, rain, and snow, but I wouldn't have refused if it meant a couple of hours alone with him.

'Okay, you're on. But don't worry, I'm not going anywhere job-wise. I know my position at St Bride's is a bit unconventional, but the stress is nothing compared to what I went through in my old life. The terms are short, the holidays long, and the accommodation is hard to beat.' He locked his eyes on mine. 'As is the company.'

I felt myself being played, and I wasn't going to let Joe off the hook so easily.

I perched on the arm of his chair, pretending to read the main news item on the front page over his shoulder – a dull story about a planning permission feud between a local farmer and the council. I recognised it from checking out the newspaper's website the night before. To my annoyance, I'd found they had already uploaded the new edition to the website, and the previous week's was no longer available. My only alternative had been to search their news archives, hoping they'd have added that issue's content already. But the website's search function had been so clunky as to be almost unusable, and after a few fruitless searches under the school's name, it had frozen altogether and the whole site had crashed. Oriana had said the paper was run on a shoestring budget, and it clearly didn't allow for competent IT support.

While he was off his guard, I tried to catch him out about our encounter the previous evening.

'By the way, did you manage to find Oriana last night?'

I tried to sound as if my only concern was solving his problem.

'What? Oh, yes. Thank you.' His expression clouded for a moment. 'You see, I needed to speak to her urgently about something, and usually I'd have just phoned her from my flat, but I knew she wanted to keep her line free for a call she was expecting from Australia. But don't worry, we didn't break any school rules.' Then he brightened. 'So if you're looking for an excuse to put me in detention, you're out of luck. Although I could think of worse punishments.'

My cheeks glowed at his flirtatious reply, and I glanced around the staffroom to check whether anyone was listening.

I was out of luck. Oriana was heading towards us, her eyes fixed on Joe.

Joe leapt up and went to meet her, presumably to prevent me hearing whatever she had to say to him. I threw myself down into Joe's vacated armchair, still warm from his body, and picked up his discarded newspaper, straining my ears to tune into their conversation. To my frustration, Oriana led Joe by the elbow to the furthest corner of the staffroom again. There was no hope of eavesdropping now.

Opening the newspaper at random, I was immediately distracted by a neat hole in page seven, the size of a picture postcard, from which a story had been excised with surgical precision. This time it was on the social pages. A chilling thought ran through me. Perhaps there was simply a running story on a budding romance between two St Bride's teachers, so often seen around town together these days?

It was more than I could bear to verify my guess by looking up the online version of the newspaper. If Oriana and Joe had decided to make a spectacle of themselves, I was not going to demean myself by intervening.

9

PLAYING BY THE BOARD

The next Sunday, when I was due to have my date with Joe, couldn't come quick enough for me. School-wide essential life skills sessions on the Saturday afternoon proved a welcome distraction, making the day fly by.

Felicity Button had procured enough sets of the games chosen by the staff to ensure every pupil was catered for. With the help of a team of prefects, she had filled the hall and the gymnasium with the small single desks used for exams. Pushed together in pairs and covered with squares of forest-green felt, these made good card tables. On each one lay either a board game or a pack of playing cards.

In the library, Mavis had solved her scrap paper shortage by repurposing old exam question papers, printed on only one side, tearing them lengthways against a ruler into three strips. Along with a pot of pens on every table, these were all she needed to teach the girls to play Consequences.

With her customary efficiency, Felicity had put on to a spreadsheet a complex timetable allowing the girls to move between rooms, so that each would have the opportunity to learn two games that afternoon. Every Saturday until half term, the exeat weekend excluded, this process would be repeated, so that by the time they went home on Valentine's Night, they'd be brimming with new game skills to share with their families and friends over the holidays. Hairnet predicted that parents would be thrilled when the girls went home requesting chess sets and dominoes rather than computer games.

In the Trough, immediately after Saturday lunch, each girl was told her timetable for the afternoon. The girls on my lunch table were due to start by learning Scrabble with me in the gymnasium, a part of the school I had barely set foot in until then. As we entered Joe's territory, the girls had to remind me to remove my outdoor shoes. The dove-grey, vinyl, sprung floor rebounding beneath my tread came as a pleasant surprise after the unyielding gleaming oak parquet and flagstones in the old part of the school. This state-of-the-art-flooring provided a safer, softer landing for young gymnasts than the hard wooden boards of the old gym, now demolished, built in the days when PE meant lining up in rows for synchronised exercises in leotards and country dancing in beribboned skirts.

Once the girls had settled at the three tables set aside for Scrabble, they eagerly opened the boxes and spread out the boards. Before I could stop them, one of the groups had tipped all the letter tiles onto the table and started arranging them face up in alphabetical order. Poppy was reading the instruction sheet with a puzzled frown.

'So where are the clues? Crosswords are hard enough *with* clues, but surely you're not expecting us to do one without them? That would be like trying to do a jigsaw puzzle without looking at the picture on the box.'

Imogen gave her a pitying look. 'It's not a crossword puzzle, silly. It's a word game. You choose what words to put down according to what letters you pick. They don't give you clues.'

Poppy began to rummage through the jumble of tiles in the middle of the table, to the irritation of the girls bent on alphabetising them all. With a triumphant flourish, she picked out three tiles and set them down in a row in the middle of the board.

'I can do BUM!' she cried, to the amusement of her friends.

The other girls on her table fell about laughing, jogging the table and making the tiles rattle.

'No, no,' said Viola. 'Miss Lamb, tell her she has to wait her turn!'

Similar scenarios were playing out on the other two Scrabble tables, amid a clamour of questions and well-meaning advice.

'So do we start by putting the first word in the top left corner, like you do when writing on paper?'

'No, silly, because this a board, not a piece of paper.'

'Can we go diagonally? It looks like it wants you to go diagonally, with all these nice coloured squares running criss-cross. You get extra points when you put words on those squares, look!'

I clapped my hands for attention.

'Girls, girls! I appreciate your enthusiasm, but let's not try to run before we can walk.'

That confused them. Served me right for speaking in clichés. An English teacher should know better.

'What I mean is, you need to know the rules before you start playing. Hands up if any of you have ever played Scrabble before.'

Three hands went up from girls on the more orderly table.

'Okay, now, let's shuffle you up a little,' I said. 'I want an experienced player in each group to coach the others.'

'Shuffle us? We're not a pack of cards, Miss.'

'We're not like the playing card soldiers in *Alice in Wonderland*.'

Ignoring the hecklers, two of the three girls who'd raised their hands scraped their chairs back and went to sit at other tables.

'Look, Miss, now we're playing musical chairs!' cried Poppy.

Joe, supervising Cluedo nearby, called across to me, 'Nice multi-tasking, Miss Lamb! Three games at once!'

My girls giggled, but I didn't let him put me off.

'Now, each pick a letter from the bag. Close your eyes! No peeking! Closest to "A" goes first.'

Tilly held up her chosen tile – a blank.

'Oh no, my letter has fallen off. Look, my tile's empty.'

She slipped off her chair to search on the floor for her missing letter, running her palms over the vinyl beneath the shade of the green felt tablecloth.

'Maybe it's rubbed off onto a different tile,' suggested Eliza. 'Has anyone picked a tile with two letters on?'

'Is that what these double letter scores mean, Miss? You need to put a tile on with two letters on it?'

Hairnet was right: teaching the girls the rudiments of popular games would spare them embarrassment in social situations.

Thankfully, young minds learned fast, especially when the spirit was willing. Once they'd allowed me to explain the rules, the girls soon started to get the hang of the game, placing interesting and clever words on the board – though not always accurately spelled.

Viola tugged at my sleeve while awaiting her turn.

'Miss Lamb,' she said, 'my granddad makes jokes I don't understand when we play Scrabble at home. Why does he say "Can I have a wee, please, Bob?"'

I bit my lip to hide a smile.

'He's referring to a different game. Have you heard of an old television game show called *Blockbusters*? My parents were huge fans in the eighties, and we'd play a version of it for a Christmas parlour game. The contestants had to choose a particular letter, and the question master, Bob Holness, would ask them a question whose answer began with that letter. I expect what your granddad actually says is, "I'll have a 'P' please, Bob." That was a bit of a running joke in the show.'

The girls shrieked in delight, the tiles on their boards shifting as they thumped the tables in their mirth.

'Miss Spryke, Miss Spryke! Miss Lamb said "pee"!'

Joe strolled across to join the fun. 'Miss Lamb, really! We can't take you anywhere!'

Emboldened by the jovial atmosphere, I edged up to him and said in a low voice that only he could hear above the racket, 'But don't let that put you off our date tomorrow.'

He took a tiny step closer and nudged his shoulder against mine. The unexpected physical contact made me shiver with anticipation.

10

LADY OF THE MANOR

So successful was that first games afternoon that some of the girls continued playing in their free time after supper. I even had to confiscate a pack of cards that Veronica, who had spent the second half of the afternoon in Max's group, had taken to bed with her, just in case she could tempt anyone to a game of poker if they woke up in the night.

I was looking forward to swapping stories about the girls' games with my colleagues after breakfast on Sunday. Mavis had promised to save the results of her girls' games of Consequences to share with us. It seemed inevitable that some girls would nominate staff names as the two characters at the start of each game, with hilarious results. I started to invent one of my own: *Joe Spryke met Gemma Lamb at St Bride's School...*

My pleasant daydream was cut short when an anxious-looking Joe caught up with me as I was heading from the Trough to the staffroom. With one hand on the small of my back, he steered me gently into the deserted library for privacy. As he pulled out a chair and beckoned for me to sit down, I realised from his clouded expression that he was about to break bad news. When he perched on the table beside me, I realised how the girls must feel when a teacher settles down with them to critique their work.

He sighed before he spoke.

'There's no way to sugar-coat this, Gemma, but I'm afraid I'll have to bunk off our date this afternoon.'

Avoiding his eyes, I stared out of the window and down to the lake. The distraught cry of a passing peacock echoed my feelings. I pressed my lips together to help me hold back my tears, and said nothing, mindful of the old maxim about the power of silence. Sure enough, Joe kept talking to fill the void.

'Honestly, Gemma, I promise you there's nothing I'd like better than to spend this afternoon with you, but Oriana has organised something that I absolutely have to do, and now is the only time it can be done.'

My feathered spokesman, strutting across the snow-speckled lawn, became increasingly blurred as I willed the tears not to fall.

'Gemma, I'm so sorry. I'll make it up to you next Wednesday, I swear. I'll give you the best afternoon off ever.'

I shrugged.

'Well, what Oriana wants...'

I broke off, realising how petulant that sounded. It was the sort of thing one of the less mature Year 7s might have said when not getting her own way. I touched the corners of my eyes with my fingertips and wiped them dry on my woollen sweater. I tried again.

'Okay, that's no problem. Don't worry about me, I've plenty here to amuse myself.'

I was lying. For once, the gardens, drenched in drizzle, looked uninviting. A dull day indoors on my own loomed large.

Joe smiled, but his eyes stayed sad.

'If you get bored, I'm sure you can find a few willing volunteers for a game of scrabble.'

'All the girls have signed up for outings. Anyway, with the luck I'm having today, they'd probably beat me hollow.' I forced a smile. 'That would dent my authority as their English teacher.'

Joe eased himself off the table and stretched his arms above his head. As he clasped his hands for a long stretch, his sweatshirt rode up a few centimetres, and I tried not to think how taut his belly would be beneath his T-shirt.

'If they do, just tell them you let them win, following Hairnet's instructions,' Joe was saying. I sat up straighter, trying to concentrate on his words rather than his body. 'No need to lose face.'

'Hmm, that's a good line: "I meant to lose." Did you ever try it in your athletics career?' As soon as I'd said it, I wished I hadn't spoken. It was a stupid thing to say. 'You're right, though,' I tried to redeem myself. 'When my grandma taught me to play scrabble, she used to lose on purpose sometimes to encourage me. I didn't realise until I had grown-up, when it was too late to thank her, even though as a child I wondered how such an intelligent person could sometimes find only three-letter words.'

Joe smiled. 'That's very cute. So what was the best word any of your girls came up with yesterday?'

'Believe it or not, I thought one of them attempted "acquiescence".'

'Wow! They must have a good English teacher.'

I grinned. 'You'd think so. Except she spelled it "a-q-u-a-s-e-n-s-e", and when one of the other girls challenged it, it became clear she thought it meant water-divining.'

We both laughed more than her error merited.

When I scraped back my chair, Joe jumped to his feet.

'Come on,' he said, patting my shoulder. 'I've just got time to divine us a cup of coffee in the staffroom before I have to go out.' At least he did me the courtesy of omitting 'with Oriana', but I still thought it all the same.

11

ENTER BUTTONS

That afternoon, with all of the girls and staff off campus on outings to museums, the cinema, or the local shopping mall, St Bride's felt strangely quiet, especially compared to Saturday's raucous games afternoon. Of course, I could have gone out in my car by myself but the dismal weather put me off.

After I'd waved the minibuses of girls from the forecourt, I'd decided that I'd just stoke up the fire in my flat and brace myself to tackle the local newspaper website again. Clearly no one else in the staffroom was going to tell me what it was we weren't meant to know about, but I'd teach them to tease me about my sleuthing skills. I wasn't going to allow Oriana, Joe, or anyone else to cover up some controversy that might threaten the school – or my job.

Then a moment after the last minibus had left the drive, a car I didn't recognise had appeared on the horizon. With Max off campus accompanying the museum trip, I decided I'd better check out the unexpected visitor myself for security reasons.

The car was a sporty little convertible, its pistachio-green bodywork and caramel leather roof pretty and fresh against the muddy pastureland either side of the drive, now dotted with pools of standing water from the thaw. It was just as well Joe had gone out by car with Oriana rather on his bike, or he'd be covered in mud before he left campus. Fleetingly, I felt the bigger person for considering his well-being over my hurt feelings.

This selfless thought was swiftly followed by wishing Joe had a smart little car like the visitor's, rather than a bicycle. Cycling through quiet country lanes had been delightful on warm, dry autumn days, but driving about in a sporty little number with the top down would be much nicer. Then I remembered how I had been critical of my ex for investing in a fancy car for the sake of vanity. Goodness, was I turning into Oriana, placing wealth above personality?

As the car drew to a halt on the forecourt, I narrowed my eyes to get a better view of the driver. Was it someone I knew? Perhaps it was one of the girls' parents or the friend of a colleague...

The driver's door swung open, and a trim, elegant man in neat chinos, shiny chestnut brogues, and a grey marl tweed jacket unfolded himself from the low-slung seat, stood up, and stretched. With one hand on the roof of the car, and the other on top of the open door, he gazed about himself with the air of someone visiting an old haunt and needing to refamiliarize himself with its layout.

Then I realised he'd spotted me lurking beneath the portico, where I'd remained to avoid the chilly drizzle now beginning to fall. With arms wrapped round myself for warmth, I strolled across the gravel to speak to him.

'Hello, how can I help you?'

Hairnet had trained us to use this as our standard opener on the phone and in person, rather than the more straightforward 'Can I help you?', which, she observed, suggested the possibility that we might not be able to help the caller at all.

The fair-haired man smiled, his cheeks dimpling as he held out his hand for me to shake. Despite the cold, his hand was toasty warm. I liked him immediately.

'How do you do?' he said. This old-fashioned greeting from one so young made me immediately classify him as posh. He looked about thirty – probably too young to be the father of a pupil, and likely too old to be an older brother, unless there was a huge age gap between them. 'I'm looking for some information about someone connected with St Bride's.'

'Do you mean a pupil or a member of staff?'

Could this be a journalist on Joe's trail? Had a reporter finally tracked him down in his hideaway at St Bride's? Or was he following up whatever story it was that had been censored from the school copy of the local paper? Perhaps I didn't need to resort to my laptop to research the story after all. Here was the journalist on the trail of rumour and scandal – and my chance to find out first-hand exactly what the story was that he was pursuing.

I was wary of giving away more than the visitor already knew.

'Not a teacher,' he continued. 'More of an associate.'

So was it Max he was after? Max kept his past confidential. Perhaps he'd rather keep his whereabouts private also.

The rain began to fall more heavily, so for my own sake as much as for his, I beckoned the man to join me under the portico.

'I'm really sorry, but I'm quite new here, and I have neither the authority nor the knowledge to answer questions about human resources. It would be better if you emailed your query to the bursar. You can easily reach him via the contact form on our website. All the messages go straight to him. They won't be weeded out and discarded by a secretary, if that's what's worrying you.'

The visitor wrinkled his perfectly formed nose, reminding me strangely of how Oriana expressed her displeasure when thwarted. One of the non-verbal ways, anyway.

'To be honest, I've tried that several times over the last few months, but he's never replied.'

The man fiddled with the collar of the pristine cream linen shirt beneath his tweed jacket. Now I found myself wanting to protect the bursar too.

'We have just had a month's break for the Christmas holidays, so he's probably still catching up with his emails.'

The visitor put his head on one side, birdlike, inquisitive.

'Are you sure you can't help? Could you please at least introduce me to one of your colleagues who might know more? The headmistress, perhaps?'

As I hesitated, distrustful of his motives, he stepped out from beneath the portico to peer up at the building's façade. The usually honey-coloured stone had been dulled by the rain. All the rooms lay in darkness. As usual, just before the mass Sunday afternoon exodus, the bursar would have run round the building flicking all the light switches off, taking every opportunity to pare down the school's enormous electricity bill.

'Unless you're the only one about the place,' the visitor added. 'Where are you hiding all the staff and girls?'

'Oh, they're out on trips this afternoon.'

As soon as I'd said it, I realised how unwise it was to reveal my solitude. What had struck me as welcome calm when the minibuses departed now began to feel like eerie silence. There was no one within shouting distance, with the possible exception of Hairnet, who would most likely be tucked away in her private apartment listening to classical music. I couldn't expect much help from that quarter. For the first time that term, I felt vulnerable and isolated. I might as well have been at the North Pole.

The visitor smiled. 'Home alone, eh, Cinderella?'

The whimsical fairy-tale reference made me smile back, but it did not make me lower my guard, even though there was something familiar about him that helped put me at my ease. I wasn't sure what.

'How about I play the fairy godmother and take you out for afternoon tea?'

When he glanced at his car, my eyes followed his, and I realised I was longing to find out just how comfortable those caramel leather seats were. (Soft as down, I was soon to discover.)

Besides, hadn't my supposed boyfriend just fobbed me off – again – so that he could spend the afternoon with another woman? If he wasn't treating our relationship as exclusive, why should I?

Because it would be reckless to get into a stranger's car, that's why, I admonished myself. I was being no less naïve than a child accepting sweets from a stranger in the park, or an invitation to go back to his house to see some kittens.

Then out of the corner of my eye I saw Hairnet coming out on to the portico, McPhee at her heels. If this man really was a rumour-mongering journalist in search of dirt on the school, I needed to protect Hairnet from him at all costs.

'They do excellent scones at the hotel where I'm staying,' the man was saying. 'It would be no trouble at all to drop you back here again afterwards.'

My desire to protect St Bride's overcame my instinct to resist.

'Thank you, Buttons, that would be grand.'

His face lit up.

As he handed me into the front passenger seat, I tried to calm my anxiously beating heart by picturing Lord Bunting helping his wife into their carriage decades before on this very spot. Was it Lord Bunting that the stranger reminded me of? I shot a sideways glance at him. No, he was nothing like the portrait in the hall. One of the governors, perhaps? When I'd met them all in my first term at St Bride's, they'd exuded the same kind of old-fashioned courtesy. Nope, I drew a blank there too.

As he started the near-silent engine and steered the car gently around the turning circle towards the drive, I sat back nervously to await my fate.

12

THE SHREW'S NEAR MISS

Only when he turned right past the bursar's gatehouse lodge, rather than left by Max's, did it occur to me that we might be heading to The Excelsior Hotel in Cirencester, and the famed Doilies tearoom beloved of the girls – too expensive to be a regular haunt for St Bride's staff. At least there we'd be in a public place, where I could easily scream for help or make a dash for it. I wondered how realistic it would be to excuse myself to go to the Ladies and make a surreptitious escape through the window. I hoped the Ladies had a window.

Whenever I ventured out for afternoon tea with Joe, we usually didn't go further than the pub or the bookshop in the nearby village of Wendlebury Barrow. This wasn't only so we didn't waste too much of our precious time off by driving long distances; it was also because their menus were relatively cheap. So it was double the treat to be taken to Doilies at the expense of this pleasant stranger, who, judging from his car and his expensive clothes, could easily afford to treat me.

As we drove along, I kept sneaking glances at him out of the corner of my eye. There was something strangely neutral about his appearance. I could imagine him blending in with any social situation, a master of disguise. He reminded me of one of those actors who can morph into any role that comes their way, like Gary Oldman or Ralph Fiennes. I could as easily picture him in a dinner suit at a formal ball as in a quirky T-shirt and board shorts on a beach in Australia. I really ought to find out more about him. I took the easy route into investigation by first telling him about myself.

'I'm Gemma Lamb, by the way.' I turned to watch his reaction. 'My job title is head of English, but really I'm only a teacher. I don't have much influence in the school, compared to the bursar.'

He smiled without looking at me. 'Don't say "only". Schools would be nothing without teachers. I'm Oliver Galsworthy, and I'm a journalist.'

So I was right to be guarded.

He removed his right hand from the steering wheel and offered it to me to shake my cold, clammy hand.

'Galsworthy, like the Edwardian author of *The Forsyte Saga*? How wonderful. I've never met a Galsworthy before.'

He shot me a mischievous look.

'Well, I have the advantage over you then,' he said. 'I've met plenty of lambs.'

I couldn't help but laugh. He was proving to be easy company, but I told myself to be wary of a charm offensive. Still, two could play at that game.

'So, Oliver Galsworthy, are you related to the more famous John?'

He shrugged. 'I've a few famous relatives, but I don't think he is one of them. Actually, it's one of my famous forebears I've come to research.'

'Four bears? Then you're one up on Goldilocks!'

'I'd rather take a lamb out to tea than a bear any day. Besides, I don't suppose Doilies have porridge on their menu after 10 a.m., even on a Sunday.'

Ah, so we were definitely going to Doilies. I rested my left elbow contentedly on the windowsill and began to enjoy the ride.

As he slowed down in Tetbury's Church Street to allow some pedestrians to cross the road, he raised a forefinger from the steering wheel to point at the historic Market House, raised high on stone columns.

'Remarkable architecture round here in these little Cotswold market towns. All warm and soft, almost fuzzy at the edges, like an Edward Ardizzone illustration. No wonder my father loved it so.'

'Your father? So is he the forebear you're researching?'

Perhaps his father was related to a contemporary of Lord Bunting's. That would be nothing to worry about. Anything that happened so long ago could hardly pose a threat to the school's reputation.

He negotiated the corner onto Long Street.

'Yep, the late, great Piers Galsworthy,' he confirmed.

Piers Galsworthy! Not the man that Hairnet had her fling with? Surely there couldn't be two people of that unusual name associated with St Bride's?

He took my horrified silence for indifference.

'I suppose he wasn't the sort of fellow to impress an English teacher. His fame was City-based. He was a phenomenal entrepreneur and a business leader of his day. A captain of industry, you might say. He'd have been even more well-known if he hadn't died relatively young, in his fifties.'

I felt torn between fear and sympathy.

'I'm sorry for your loss, Oliver,' I said cautiously, dreading what else he might come out with. After all, Piers Galsworthy was the married man with whom Hairnet had had an affair that had resulted in Oriana's birth and the transfer of ownership of the school estate to Hairnet in compensation. But this must stay a closely guarded secret to preserve the school's reputation.

He shifted up a gear as we accelerated away from Tetbury, bowling along the road towards Cirencester.

'Thank you, but it's not exactly a fresh or open wound. I never knew him. He died when I was a baby.'

So he hadn't picked up his chivalrous manners from his father.

'My mother married again shortly afterwards,' he continued, 'to a very pleasant fellow, a successful architect by trade, one Colin Blenkinsop. He raised me as his own, so I can't complain. But there comes a time, you know, when one wonders about one's roots. Hitting a certain age, if you get my drift.'

I tried to lighten the mood again.

'That pesky twenty-one, eh?'

He guffawed.

'Thirty, if you must know, as of last March. Ever since then, I've had the urge to find out more about my real father, before I settle down to have children of my own, or at least find someone who might become the mother of my children eventually.'

His eyes met mine in the rear-view mirror.

'Not that you're anywhere near that age yourself. Still footloose and fancy free, I suppose?'

The casual tone of his voice didn't deceive me. He was sounding me out. Was that my fault for leading him on by accepting his invitation to go out to tea?

'Not exactly fancy free, I'm afraid. While romantic relationships between colleagues are not exactly encouraged at St Bride's, I'm in the early stages of one with a fellow member of staff. But it's completely hush-hush during termtime.'

Oliver raised his eyebrows in mock horror.

'How scandalous!'

I laughed. 'The girls would have a field day teasing us if they knew. Especially—'

I clapped my hand to my mouth before I could say another word. I could hardly believe I'd been about to reveal Joe's secret identity to a stranger, who might, for all I knew, still prove to be a tabloid reporter out to muckrake about Joe's past.

The story about Oliver's famous father could have been a smoke-screen, and his flattering manner a cynical ploy to win my confidence. Or perhaps, worse still, he was a would-be abductor, come to case the joint before whisking one of our girls away. I gasped.

'Gemma, are you okay?'

He laid a hand gently on my arm.

I thought quickly. 'Sorry, Oliver, I just saw a shrew run out in front of the car. I thought we were going to hit it, but it was too quick for us. Phew!'

Oliver's shoulders relaxed.

'Thank goodness! You had me worried for a moment. I can't bear killing harmless creatures.'

I sank down in my seat. That was just the sort of thing an attacker might say to put their potential victim off their guard. I glanced down at the passenger door to locate the handle, in case I needed to make a sudden escape. I wished I'd paid more attention to the last question on the Year 10's maths worksheet when I'd covered their lesson for Oriana: if an object falls from a vehicle moving at fifty miles per hour, at what speed is it travelling when it hits the ground?

13

TEA AND SYMPATHY

I was glad to see the sign indicating we were entering Cirencester. It had never occurred to me before how sparsely populated the road was between here and Tetbury. There was barely a building where one might seek help if abandoned or ejected or escaping from a car along the way.

Fortunately, Oliver seemed oblivious to my discomfort, merely remarking on the attractiveness of the grand parish church of St John Baptist as we headed along the marketplace towards Dyer Street. He wondered whether his father had ever attended services or concerts there. His relaxed demeanour put me at ease once more. Of course, his intentions were innocent. I really ought to stop jumping to false conclusions on flimsy evidence.

Only when we were settling into Doilies' crimson velvet and gilt chairs did he resume his questioning.

'So how long have you been a teacher at St Bride's?'

He passed me a menu and I glanced at it as I replied.

'I was new last term,' I explained. 'This is my first academic year.'

Oliver nodded thoughtfully behind his menu. Then when a grey-haired waitress in a lace-edged white apron materialised beside us, Oliver smiled sweetly up at her.

'Please may I have the Cotswold cream tea, with damson jam and the Bibury blend?'

I was finding it hard to concentrate on the menu, so I took the easy option.

'The same for me, please.'

The waitress smiled politely as she gently relieved us of our menus before drifting silently away.

'So, as I was saying, I was a baby when my father died. Now I'm writing his biography as a way of getting to know him.'

'So do you write books as well as being a journalist?'

Oliver leaned back in his chair, palms on his thighs, as the waitress laid delicate ivory-coloured porcelain crockery and ornate silver knives and teaspoons in front of us.

'Here.' He reached into his inside jacket pocket a slim leather card-case and pulled out a business card naming him as a staff writer for a magazine I'd never heard of. Of course, it could have been a fake. These days, anyone could design a business card for a bogus company and get it printed and delivered within days by an online service. It proved nothing.

'Yes, sorry, didn't I say? I work for the magazine, but I also ghost-write memoirs for a commercial publishing company. I suppose that experience plus my journalistic training makes writing a book about my father the natural way for me to find out more about him. I want to delve below the surface of the superficial obituaries published on his death. A psychiatrist might say I'm trying to prolong my father's life by reviving him in print, to compensate for my sense of his abandoning me as a baby.' He picked up his teaspoon and began to trace the fine pattern on the handle with his fingertip. 'But I don't care. Psychiatrists can say what they like about me.'

He set the spoon on his saucer and leaned forward.

'All I know is,' he continued, 'I feel so much better for having traced his story so far. More complete, you might say.'

The waitress glided up beside us again, this time with a well-oiled silver trolley, and transferred on to the centre of our table a loaded cake stand. On the bottom of the three plates sat four plump scones, with dishes of gleaming dark-red and purple jams on the middle one, and tiny saucers of butter-yellow clotted cream on top. Next she set down a large lace-patterned teapot, milk jug, and sugar bowl, along with a dainty silver tea-strainer on a matching dish.

'Real tea leaves!' I sighed contentedly. 'What a treat.'

Allowing the tea to brew, we helped ourselves to scones. Then I poured for us both, careful to avoid splashing the tar-coloured tea on to the brilliant-white lace tablecloth. And yes, there were doilies on the cake stand, and not just disposable paper ones, but starched white mats crocheted in the finest cotton thread. At that moment, I wouldn't have swapped this experience for afternoon tea with Joe at Hector's House.

I set down the teapot. 'So, are you researching your father's story in chronological order?'

I was genuinely interested. After spending Christmas rebuilding my relationship with my own parents, I was starting to feel sorry for this half-orphaned man, and I was intrigued by his coping mechanism of writing a biography.

He swallowed a mouthful of tea.

'Yes, it seemed the simplest way to go about it. Last spring, I revisited his birthplace and the landmarks of his childhood. Most adults who would have known him in his youth are dead now, of course – his school-teachers, scoutmaster, that sort of thing – so I could only get a child's perspective from his old schoolfriends. Then in the summer, I moved on to his university and military years. He joined the army straight from university and served for twelve years before entering the world of industry at executive level, which was common practice in those days. In September I started unravelling his career in commerce, which was pretty meteoric. By the time I came along he was already set up for life, working fewer hours and able to "pay it forward", as we'd call it now, although I don't think he'd have used that term. So now I'm exploring that aspect of his life.'

I helped myself to another scone. Scones could be stodgy, but these were marshmallow-light.

'His charitable work, do you mean?'

Oliver lifted the teapot to refill our cups, as I held the tea strainer in place over each cup in turn.

'Exactly. I'm interested to know more about the charities he engaged with, why he chose them, and what his contribution was in practical terms, not just how much money he gave, although I'm sure he donated from his own purse too. I'm fascinated to find out why he became involved with a traditional girls' boarding school when his career was in engineering. A technical college or university, I could understand, but this...'

'Oh, that's easy.' I set the tea strainer in its silver dish and added milk to our cups. 'The Bunting connection. The founder of St Bride's was a famous Victorian engineer. That probably made your father feel a kindred spirit. I can tell you all about Bunting. He's the stuff of school legend.'

Perhaps if I could give him enough information about Bunting to satisfy his curiosity and send him on his way.

Oliver topped his second scone with cream.

'Yes, that makes sense,' he said. 'Besides, his excellent business acumen could be applied to any kind of enterprise, including a school. Although what strikes me as odd is that during his tenure as chair, he wound up the charity that used to run it. My father never failed at anything else, so I'm wondering what went wrong. To be honest, I'm a little nervous of finding out, because otherwise I'm proud of everything he achieved. I'm worried he left St Bride's under a cloud. Not long afterwards, he died. Perhaps his failure at the school adversely affected his health. It might even have been something so scandalous that it made him take his own life. His death was very sudden. That would explain why my mother was always so averse to talking about him. Her instinct must have been to protect me.'

He laid his hands flat on the table and stared at the loaded scone on his plate. Instinctively, I covered his hands with my own to comfort him.

'Oh, but the school went on to thrive. It wasn't as if he shut it down. He just arranged for a transfer of ownership from the charity to the head-mistress. She's been running it ever since, and it's doing fine.'

When I'd begun to speak, I'd been confident that by glossing over the reasons for the transfer – the affair between his father and Hairnet – I might put his mind at rest and deter him from making any further enquiries. But as my words tailed off, I realised for the first time why I'd taken to Oliver so readily. With his fine-boned face, exquisite manners and neutral features, he reminded me exactly of someone I knew well: Oriana Bliss. Of course, he must be Oriana's half-brother.

14

RELATIVE MATTERS

I'd been hoping to get the chance to catch up with Joe before the girls returned, to tell him about my outing and to gauge his opinion on how to handle Oliver. But to my acute discomfort, when Oliver pulled on to the forecourt to drop me back at school, the only person about was Hairnet. She had just opened the front door, ready to welcome back the minibuses of girls, due to return at any minute, and was sheltering under the portico. The rain was falling more heavily now, and thankfully she was standing right at the back, on the doorstep, almost concealed by shadows.

Hairnet was the last person I wanted Oliver to meet. I needed time to decide how to answer his enquiries diplomatically and accurately without upsetting Hairnet, Oriana, or anyone else, and without losing my job for indiscretion, like my predecessor. It was important he remained in the car now and went on his way.

As I unclipped my seatbelt, Oliver went to unfasten his too. I put my hand out to stop him.

'Don't worry about seeing me in,' I said hastily. 'You'll only get wet. The rain's a lot heavier than when we left Cirencester. But thanks for a lovely afternoon. It was so interesting to meet you and hear about your family. I'll do my best to find out more information about your father, and I'll email it to you.'

I still hadn't decided whether I would tell him anything at all, but for now my priority was to send him on his way before Hairnet spotted him and before Oriana returned. Even though they hadn't met, he'd doubtless recognise Hairnet from the school website. She might even recognise him, if he looked anything like his father. I assumed Hairnet must know of Oliver's existence, but I wondered whether Piers' widow knew about Oriana, or even of her husband's affair with Hairnet. Blended families were the norm these days, but had Piers survived, theirs would have been an awkward mix. I was glad my own family life was so simple and straightforward.

I leapt out of the car before Oliver could protest and inadvertently slammed the heavy door behind me. As I trudged across the wet gravel, several shades darker for the downpour, I was relieved to realise Hairnet had retreated inside. I lingered to watch Oliver swing his car around the turning circle, tooting his horn in a cheerful farewell. As he entered the drive, he opened his window and stuck out his hand in a final goodbye gesture. I waved back and watched the retreating car until it disappeared out of sight beyond the gatehouses.

What a pleasant afternoon it had turned out to be, despite my initial misgivings. If things didn't work out between me and Joe, then perhaps...

I slipped my hand into my jacket pocket and touched the corners of the slate-grey business card that Oliver had slid across the table to me, conveying his mobile number and email address. Had I seen the last of him? The choice was mine.

But what was I thinking? Quite apart from risking my relationship with Joe, what better way to alienate Hairnet than to strike up a relationship with the legitimate son of the father of her illegitimate daughter? Whether or not Oriana knew of Oliver's existence – he certainly didn't appear to know of her – it was not for me to stir things up. And I wanted to keep my job and my staff flat.

Realising I had got very wet, I made a dash for the entrance hall.

'He looked a pleasant young man, my dear.'

Miss Harnett's voice at the foot of the marble staircase startled me.

'Lovely car, too,' she said, narrowing her eyes. 'I had thought there was something shaping up between you and dear Joe? I of all people know how careful one must be with relationships in school, and I was thinking only this morning – with gratitude, my dear – how discreet you and Joe have been. Or have I mistaken the absence of a relationship for discretion?'

Talk about being put on the spot. I chose my words carefully so as not to reveal Oliver's identity. The last thing I wanted was to arouse her curiosity.

'Joe and I enjoy each other's company, and we shared some pleasant outings last term,' I began.

Hairnet dipped her chin and raised her eyebrows, waiting for me to say more. I could imagine her using the same body language to extract confessions from naughty girls. I continued speaking before I had consciously thought of what to say.

'And we had a lovely couple of days away together over the Christmas holidays. The fellow I've been out with this afternoon is just a friend. A friend who happened to be down this way with an hour or two to spare, and he called by on the off chance.' Well, he was a friend now. I was telling the truth, if not the whole truth. 'I had planned to go out with Joe, but Joe had to be elsewhere. So, when my friend invited me to afternoon tea at Doilies, it would have seemed churlish to refuse.'

Hairnet beamed approval. 'Is your friend single? If so, when he visits again, you might like to introduce him to Oriana. You know what she's like about cars. She'd love to go for a spin in a sporty little number like that.' Her eyes twinkled, even in the dim light of the entrance hall. 'So much healthier for her to date someone closer to her age who is uncon-nected with the school, don't you think? She might also find more in common with someone like him than with one of the girls' fathers.'

So close in age they're practically twins, I thought. And sharing half their genetic material gave them more in common than Hairnet could possibly guess.

'Sadly, they're about the only unattached men she seems able to meet, living and working where she does,' Hairnet continued.

There was me thinking that the worst gaffe I could make was to intro-duce Hairnet to her dead lover's legitimate son. Fixing up a blind date for her daughter with her half-brother would trump that any day. For the first time since that morning, I was glad Oriana had gone out with Joe – although I still had no idea what she was up to with him.

15

A SECRET HISTORY

As the first minibus entered the drive, I darted up the stairs to grab a few minutes alone in my flat to think about how to proceed with Oliver.

The easiest way to protect Hairnet and the school would be to ghost him, as the bursar seemed to have done on receipt of his emails. But having got to know Oliver a little, I'd warmed to him, and part of me wanted to help him find closure and comfort about his late father. Being surrounded at school by girls who had lost their mothers made me sensitive to what Oliver had missed out on, as did re-establishing my relationship with my own parents since breaking up with Steven.

Unlike Oliver, I knew only too well why his mother wouldn't speak to him about his father or about his role at St Bride's. Most likely she accompanied her late husband to Speech Days and concerts here. I thought about how hard it must have been for her to retain her dignity in front of her husband's illicit lover.

If Oliver had wanted to ascribe his mother's reticence to her loyalty to her second husband, that was just as well. She must have been tempted to pass Colin Blenkinsop off as Oliver's natural father as they had married so soon after Piers' death. But even if Colin had legally adopted Oliver as a baby, the truth about his parentage would have come out as soon as

Oliver needed his birth certificate to apply for his driving licence or passport.

Although Oliver had given me all his contact details, I purposely hadn't given him mine to retain control of our communications. I didn't want to undermine my feeling of safety at St Bride's, nor did I want evidence of our association on the school computer system. Of course I had my own school email address, but I had no idea how secure it was. It would not have surprised me if the bursar or Max read staff emails in the interests of safeguarding, especially after the crisis with Katie Donovan's online indiscretions.

Obviously, Oliver knew my postal address, but I didn't mind that. An old-fashioned letter – provided no one lifted it from my pigeonhole before I had the chance to collect it – would be more easily kept for my eyes only. I just hoped Joe wouldn't notice it while sorting the post. I could burn it in my fireplace after reading it, and even Max wouldn't be able to reconstruct a letter from ash.

Not that his letter would necessarily be incriminating but Hairnet might not want him around, assuming she knew of his existence.

What a difficult situation she had been in. For Piers to refuse to leave his wife for her and then to die when Oriana was a baby must have been hard enough. To know she and his wife were pregnant at the same time must have been torture for all three of them. Then there would have been obituaries in the national newspapers and the local rags, ending with condolences for his wife and their new baby. There'd have been no such acknowledgement of Hairnet's loss or of Oriana's existence. My admiration mounted for Hairnet's dignity and resolve under the most difficult of circumstances.

I wondered whether Hairnet would have swapped places with Pier's wife if she could. Somehow, I couldn't picture them settled down in a conventional family unit. St Bride's was Hairnet's home as well as her employer, the bursar as close as she was likely to get to a husband, the girls her numerous children. If I hadn't been privy to her complex history, I'd have assumed she'd planned her life this way and was happy about it.

I certainly didn't want to threaten whatever happiness she had now by raking up her troubled past.

If only Max had been on site when Oliver had arrived, then I would never have got myself into this awkward situation. I should have just rebuffed him and not got involved, but now someone might have thought I was complicit in Oliver's investigation, especially as I'd lied and told Hairnet he was my friend. I was torn between telling Max to protect the school and concealing my own badly judged behaviour that might have been enough to get me sacked. But I felt I could trust Oliver, so for the time being, I decided not to tell Max about Oliver's visit when he got back to school. It would be hard to explain my concerns without giving away sensitive information.

I resolved to make gentle enquiries about Piers Galsworthy with Judith Gosling, the head of history, whose 'Extra' was managing the school archives. The previous term she had proved a helpful and discreet source of information, so I had no hesitation in confiding in her again. Perhaps I could extract just enough information from her to satisfy Oliver and send him on his way, without compromising the school's reputation and without rekindling old rumours about Hairnet.

The safest place to approach her in confidence without risk of being overheard was in her classroom after the last lesson tomorrow. She usually stayed there marking essays after the girls shot off at the sound of the final bell to change into their mufti for the evening. In this chilly term, novelty onesies were their favourite evening wear. It made me smile on entering the Trough for supper to see an assortment of furry animals sitting around my table, representing the wildlife of every continent, from polar bears to kangaroos, from lions to pandas.

As I entered her classroom, Judith, seated at her desk, set down her red pen.

'Hi, Gemma, had a good day?'

I strolled over and perched on the desk nearest hers. St Bride's classrooms still had old-fashioned wooden desks with bench seats attached and a hole in the top right for an ink well from the days when dip pens were in daily use. Decades earlier, an extra hole had been bored at the top left corners to allow for left-handed writers to dip their pens with ease. It was a classic St Bride's blend of modern thinking and old-fashioned values to have done this and then still to have retained these vintage desks, despite dip pens now being obsolete.

'Fine, thanks, Judith. And you?'

Judith glanced down at her pile of essays.

'Not bad at all, I'm pleased to say,' she said. 'Not a single piece of prep has been handed in late, for once. Remarkable what the powers of a new year can do for the girls' self-discipline. Long may it last!' She looked up at me with a smile. 'So, what brings you to my lair tonight, Miss Lamb?'

I chewed my lip for a moment.

'Well, it's rather a delicate situation.'

'Good-oh!' She rubbed her hands together in anticipation of something juicy.

'It's about the former chair of governors, when the school was still a charity, and before ownership was transferred to Hairnet.' I chose my words carefully so as not to give anything away. I presumed the real reason for the transfer was not public knowledge, and certainly would not be recorded in the school archives. Nor did it much matter in the scheme of things, as Hairnet's legal ownership of the school had been confirmed at the end of the previous term as a result of my sleuthing activities.

'Yesterday, when everyone else was out, I happened to be the only one in school apart from Hairnet when an unexpected visitor arrived: one Oliver Galsworthy, son of the late Piers.'

Judith pressed a forefinger to her lips in thought. 'Yes, I recognise his name from his father's death notices. Born not long before his father died. Awfully sad.'

I nodded in agreement.

'So what has become of him?' Judith asked.

'He has grown up into a pleasant man who now works as a journalist and ghost-writer of other people's memoirs. He's currently researching his father's biography. Given Hairnet's aversion to journalists, I thought it best not to introduce them.'

'Very wise, Gemma. So did you send him packing without more ado?'

I averted my gaze.

'Actually, I let him take me out to afternoon tea at Doilies, but at least I got him off the premises.'

Judith raised her eyebrows. 'Treated you to Doilies, eh? I like him already!'

I grinned in agreement, and Judith laughed.

'We have to take any perks where we can find them in this job,' she said. 'Is Doilies as lovely as the girls claim?'

Already hungry for supper, my tummy rumbled at the memory of those gravity-defying scones.

'It really is. Especially when someone else is paying.' I tried to keep the conversation as light as the scones to avoid arousing suspicion. 'Oliver was very sweet too. This project is to help him find out more about the father he never knew, and to help him find himself really, before he settles down and has children of his own.'

'Goodness, are you telling me he proposed to you while he was at it? Talk about a fast worker!'

I laughed.

'No, but I liked him enough to want to help him, if I can do so without Hairnet knowing I'm in conversation with a journo, or compromising the girls' privacy. He's been researching the biography for months and has dug up everything he can find in the public domain, but I was wondering whether we have anything in the school archives we could give him without breaking any confidences or school rules? Photos of his father at school functions, articles in the school magazine, or perhaps the chairman's introduction in the school prospectus?'

Judith considered.

'The transfer only happened about thirty years ago, and I don't think Galsworthy was chair for more than about five years. I shouldn't take me long to have a rummage through the appropriate years' boxes and see what I can find. There's bound to be something. If I leave whatever I can rustle up in your pigeonhole in a sealed envelope, can you photocopy or photograph it, and return the originals straight to me? I don't care whether you email images or send him printouts, provided he understands that it's for his eyes only. If there's anything there that's not already in the public domain that he wants to reproduce in his book, he needs to secure written permission from the bursar.'

'If they're in the public domain, won't he already have found them online?'

'Only if someone bothered to post them there. Unlikely in the case of material thirty years old, as it's before the internet was used by the general public.'

'Wow, I hadn't thought of that.'

Judith sighed. 'You millennials, you make me feel old. You're almost as bad as the girls. Anyway, the history of a small school such as this one is of interest to only a tiny group of people – just school alumni, really, and they're generally only interested in their former classmates and teachers. Governors are off their radar. Poor governors, they have a thankless task. I'll do my best to find enough bits and pieces in our archives to make this poor boy happy.'

'Not so much of the poor. I get the feeling he's well-provided for. His mother remarried another successful businessman when Oliver was still a baby, and if the fancy car he drives is anything to go by, he's pretty affluent.'

Judith raised her eyebrows. 'One of the Trust Fund Brigade, eh? Now there's a catch. If I were you, I'd tell Oriana about him. The only man she seems interested in this term is Joe. A Galsworthy seems far more like her usual type. Still, leave it with me, and I'll see what I can do.'

16

TUCKED AWAY

Judith was as good as her word, and a couple of days later I found in my pigeonhole a large cardboard envelope marked 'personal' in her neat cursive script. Not wanting to remove its contents in the staffroom, where anyone might see what I was looking at, I had to content myself with peering inside. I could just glimpse a photo on the top of the bundle of assorted documents, showing a young but recognisable Miss Harnett – the very image of Oriana without any make-up or hair dye. Her hand was resting on the handle of a garden spade beside a newly planted sapling. Next to her stood a tall lean man of about fifty, wearing an expensively tailored elegant suit, his slicked-back hair greying at the temples. They stood so close together that their arms were touching from shoulder to elbow.

'Miss Lamb, are you listening?'

The bursar's voice, booming out from the centre of the staffroom, startled me so much that I gave a little shriek of surprise.

'She is now!' replied Joe from the vantage point of his usual easy chair.

'I was just saying, Gemma, can anyone explain why tuck shop takings are so low this term?'

I shrugged. This was the first I'd heard of it.

'I just wanted to see whether any of you had any insights?' the bursar continued. 'We've taken barely a quarter of the revenue we'd normally expect by this stage in the term.'

We looked at each other, shaking our heads.

'No sudden outbreak of faddy diets, as far as I'm aware, bursar,' said Oriana.

Judith raised her hand. 'I've noticed the increase in apple cores in my house's common room bin. I imagine Miss Harnett's suggestion for their New Year intentions boosted fruit sales.'

The bursar frowned.

'Yes, but apparently at the expense of other tuck. We don't make anywhere near the same margin on apples as we do on sweets because of the wastage from their short shelf life.'

Joe folded the sports supplement he'd been reading.

'Perhaps the kids are still living off their humps from the Christmas holidays,' he said.

Mavis patted her rotund tummy. 'I know I am!'

I waited for the ripple of laughter around the room to die down before I chipped in.

'I know this is my first spring term here, so I've nothing to compare it with, but might they still be eating up tuck they brought from home? I've spotted quite a few selection boxes in our junior dorm, presumably left over from Christmas.'

'One of the Year 11s kindly gave me a giant Toblerone they didn't want,' added Judith. 'You must have seen it sticking out of my pigeonhole. If anyone wants a chunk, help yourself.'

The bursar harrumphed. 'Of course, the tuck shop doesn't stock only sweets. Sales of stationery and toiletries are down too. Have the girls been spending all their pocket money outside school? I know they were on various trips last Sunday, but surely they can't all have spent every last penny in museum gift shops?'

Joe laid his newspaper on the coffee table.

'I don't know about the stationery, or the toiletries, but Veronica had her first Harrods parcel of the term at the end of last week,' he said. 'I had to carry it up the stairs on Friday, and it weighed a ton. If it was full of sweets, and she shared the contents out as per usual, that would keep at least her friends out of the tuck shop for a week or two.'

'Oh, but it wasn't full of sweets,' put in Oriana. 'I know, because I was there when she opened it. She actually seemed pleased with her parcel for once, because the contents were chosen so much more thoughtfully than before. She said so herself.'

The bursar folded his arms. 'So what was in her parcel, Oriana? If indeed that is relevant to my enquiry?'

Oriana thought for a moment. 'Don't tell Hairnet, because she won't approve, but there was a lot of make-up, plus proper cleanser, toner and moisturiser, all from good brands. A set of curling tongs and a penguin onesie. Honestly, apart from the onesie, I would have fancied half the contents myself. Quite a change from the little-girl tat her father usually sends – inflatable pink unicorns and all that sort of nonsense. It was as if a different person altogether had chosen the contents. Not as easy to share with her friends, of course, but it's about time she kept a bit more back for herself. Her father would probably have a fit if he knew how many of his gifts end up with someone else's daughter.'

Having decided that the parcel played no part in the mystery of his diminishing tuck shop profits, the bursar glazed over until Oriana had finished talking.

'Well, please be vigilant,' he said at last. 'And if you find any reason why the girls have withdrawn their custom from the tuck shop, please let me know so that I may take steps to resolve the problem.'

With head bowed in defeat, he left the staffroom, which fell quiet until he'd closed the door behind him.

Mavis was the first to break the silence.

'I hope that doesn't mean he's going to cut the girls' rations in the Trough,' she said, 'to make them fill up on sweets and other tuck shop rubbish.'

Nicolette raised her hands in a gesture of reconciliation.

'*Calme-toi*, Mavis. Ah no, he will not do that, the bursar. He may be careful with the pennies, but he will not starve the girls. No. But you must find the answer for him and make him a happy man.'

Oriana crossed the room to speak to me by the pigeonholes.

'Come on, Gemma. You're meant to be the school sleuth. Here's a nice mystery for you to solve, and here's your first clue. When you next go upstairs, can you please double-check the contents of Veronica's box? I saw her take out the packing list when she was opening the box on Friday lunchtime, and she left it on the floor, so I put it in the recycling. It'll probably still be there.'

I resented her rather patronising tone and wondered whether she was just trying to get me out of the way again so she could spend more time with Joe. Why did she want me to look at the packing list, I thought, when she'd said herself it contained no confectionery? When I glanced across to Joe to see his reaction, he looked the other way.

If they were going to close ranks like that, I wasn't going to demean myself by chasing after him like some smitten puppy.

I pressed the seal on Judith's envelope to secure it.

'Okay, sure,' I said briskly. 'I'll just have time to do that before supper.'

17

BUNGED UP

When I reached Veronica's dorm, to my surprise, the paper recycling box was empty, even though it was not the day for the council's collection. Why would anyone have taken all the scrap paper from the dorm? The girls never did their prep here, and they left everything they used for lessons in their desks in their form rooms.

Then I remembered Mavis's Consequences, and I headed for the library, where she was tearing more A4 sheets lengthwise against a brass ruler so ancient that it was marked only in inches.

'Caught in the act!' I teased her. 'Miss Brook, in the library, with the ruler.'

She favoured me with a rare smile.

'You know,' she said, 'I almost volunteered for Cluedo instead of Consequences. Cluedo was my favourite game when I was a child. One of the reasons I came to work here, in fact – St Bride's reminded me of the country house in the board game. I was glad Hairnet designated me as librarian for my Extra, so that I could spend more time here.'

I picked up one of the paper strips and turned it over to read the used side.

'Goodness, it's a letter from home – or rather, from that girl's father who's a general serving in the Middle East.'

Mavis took the next strip from the pile and held it against mine, like a two-piece jigsaw.

'Someone should tell that child to save her father's letters. They could be of valuable historical interest in the years to come. Get Judith to have a word with her to impress on her their potential significance.'

I pointed to the word 'attack' on my strip.

'You'd think he'd know better,' I said, 'than to send sensitive security information here, but if his daughter doesn't want his old letters, we should burn or shred them rather than leave them lying about where anyone might see them.'

Mavis reached across her desk for the sticky tape dispenser and reunited my strip with hers, before holding it up to read.

'How disappointing. He's not describing a military manoeuvre, but his latest attack of gout. Hardly something to excite enemy spies. But you're right all the same. The gutter press is notorious for going through people's bins to source scandalous stories. Besides, even if the letter contains no shred of sensitive intelligence, we don't want anyone knowing that we have girls here whose parents are high up in the military. It's just inviting blackmail or kidnap.'

She folded the sheet and tucked it into her jacket pocket.

'I'll speak to the child later,' she added, 'without putting the frighteners on her, of course.'

Mavis might have seemed severe at times, but she did genuinely care for the girls' well-being.

'You know,' she mused, 'I'll always prefer physical letters to emails.' She waved a hand in the general direction of the floor-to-ceiling bookshelves which lined three sides of the library. 'Goodness knows how many of these books would never have been written without physical letters as a source of information. Well, the non-fiction, anyway. Biographies of the late and great, memoirs, collected essays.'

I wasn't going to allow myself to be diverted from my mission by one of Mavis's anti-technology lectures.

'Mavis, debating the merits of modern communication technology isn't the reason I've come to see you. It's something far more trivial. I was just looking for the delivery note that came with Veronica's latest Harrods box so that we can see exactly what was in it to stop the bursar blaming her for the drop in tuck shop revenue. Oriana told me she'd put it in the recycling box in the dorm on Friday after Veronica had left it lying about, but when I looked just now, the box was empty. I wondered whether you'd been collecting scrap paper from the dorms to use for Consequences.'

Mavis pointed at the stack of paper strips that lay on her desk before her.

'Guilty as charged. It'll be in amongst this lot somewhere. You're welcome to rummage through the pile if you like.' She checked her watch. 'I was about to pack up and go to supper anyway. I'll leave you to it.'

The Harrods packing list with its distinctive crest was easy to find. I whisked it out and put the rest of the scrap paper to one side, neatening the stack to keep the meticulous Mavis happy.

As I cast my eye down the list, I noticed how different the contents were from the babyish gifts in last term's deliveries. As Oriana had said, there were items of make-up and skincare and haircare, thoughtfully selected by someone who knew what it was like to be a self-conscious adolescent. It was highly unlikely any middle-aged man would be acquainted with the right brands for a young girl, nor with the shades to suit his daughter. The colours listed here would be perfect for Veronica, once she'd learned to apply them effectively. Although she wouldn't be allowed to wear eyeshadow or lipstick in school, I wondered whether there might be some opportunities to wear them for drama class, and certainly she could enjoy them on her weekends away.

With a few minutes to spare before the supper bell, I sprinted up the stairs to the dorm and popped the packing list in Veronica's pigeonhole as a gentle hint not to leave her things lying around. It seemed more constructive than Oriana's decision to chuck it out.

Like the staff, the girls had wooden pigeonholes in which their post and any internal mail is placed each day. The girls usually raided theirs at morning break, hoping to find a postcard from home, or a letter from penfriends overseas – another old-fashioned habit Hairnet encouraged to expand the girls' geographical and political knowledge and under-standing.

So I was surprised to see as I approached the pigeonholes outside the Year 7 dormitory that although most of them were empty, one was crammed full of scraps of paper – not correspondence from outside the school, but scruffy little notes so tightly jammed in that it was an effort to extract them. After I'd given them a couple of hard tugs, the papers came loose and a few bits fell to the floor. As I bent to pick them up, I noticed they all said pretty much the same thing:

> *To Veronica,*
>   *IOU £ (*various sums*)*
>   *Signed* (assorted girls' names)

Had Veronica been selling items from her Harrods gift box this time rather than giving them away, and accepting promissory notes in payment? As I flicked through the papers, the overall picture was clear: dozens of girls of all ages were in debt to Veronica. I entered the dorm and spread the papers out on the nearest bed for a more thorough inspection. Some notes were hastily scribbled, others written with greater care and embellished with decorations, many with the symbols of the suits in a pack of playing cards. Although most of the notes seemed innocuous, and the individual amounts relatively small, a few of them indicated the sender's bitterness. One showed a red heart at the top, with a big cross through it, written with such anger that the pen had dented the paper. The heart was prefaced with an 'I' and suffixed with a word that literally gave the game away: 'POKER'.

At the bottom was a picture of a spade, a club, and a diamond, with the caption:

> *This SPADE is what I'd like to dig your grave with, once I've CLUBBED you to death. Don't spend all your money on DIAMONDS – you're no queen of HEARTS.*

Unlike the rest, there was no signature, no value given. It was simply an expression of venom and could have been penned by any of her debtors. So much for Hairnet's theory that this term we'd be teaching all the girls to be gracious losers.

One other note stood out from the pile. It was a business card, blank on the back, until the sender had written in shaky block letters,

IOU £42. M. S.

I knew some of our older girls had printed cards for the little online businesses they ran as hobbies in their spare time, so I flipped it over to find out which girl this card belonged to.

To my surprise, printed in the flowing italic font of the school letterhead was the name, address, telephone number, and website of the school. In the white space beneath was another familiar name overprinted in khaki: 'Max Security'.

18

THE EMPTY CHAIR

The unavoidable inference was that the girls had been seized by some kind of gambling craze, with the collusion of Max, the person most responsible for their security. Unsure whether to speak first to Max, Oriana, or Veronica about my discovery, or even to escalate the situation immediately to Hairnet, I decided to wait until after supper before taking action. There was no chance Veronica or anyone else would notice the IOUs had disappeared while we were all in the Trough together. This would buy me valuable thinking time.

Taking the bundle of notes with me, I marched to the stationery cupboard to find a large envelope to put them in. Then I stuffed the notes inside and put the whole lot in my pigeonhole for safekeeping. As I crossed the hall to the Trough for supper, I hoped no one would notice my anxiety.

The usual pre-meal queue at the Trough door had dispersed by the time I got there, which meant I must be late. I hastened my step, but that was not the reason that my heart began to pound as I weaved my way between the crowded tables to my usual seat. I'd realised as soon as I saw my table that the only empty seat in the room apart from mine belonged to the child whose pigeonhole I'd just raided.

As I pulled out my chair and sat down, I forced a carefree smile.

'Well done for all being on time, girls.' I tried to sound cheerful. 'All except for Veronica, I see. Does anyone know what's keeping her?'

Nine pairs of wide eyes turned on me.

'We thought she was with you, Miss.'

'We thought she was holding you up and that's why you were late.'

'I haven't seen her since the end of geography, last lesson, Miss.'

I stared at the covered serving dishes on the table to avoid their earnest gazes.

'Perhaps she's poorly,' suggested Isobel, cheering me with the possibility of an innocent explanation for Veronica's absence. The school was too small to have a sick bay, and the usual procedure if a girl felt unwell was to alert their housemistress before taking to their bed, where they'd lie quietly until they felt better. If the child had a serious infectious illness, an empty dormitory would be used for isolation.

I scraped back my chair.

'Good idea, Isobel. I'll go and check with Miss Bliss. You carry on with supper, girls. Please help yourselves.'

'We'll help you too, Miss.'

The girl on my right took my plate and held it up for the girl beside her to load with sausages, potatoes dauphinoise, and peas.

Oriana, spotting the concern on my face, stood up as I approached her table, guessing whatever I had to tell her was best kept out of the girls' hearing. She put her hand on my arm to steer me gently to the little servery that opened off the Trough.

'What's up, Gemma? You look dreadful.'

'Oriana, have you seen Veronica since the end of lessons? She hasn't come into supper. Has she been to see you to report herself sick?'

Oriana's smooth brow furrowed.

'No, I've not seen her since lunchtime. Was she at her last lesson?'

I nodded. 'The girls said she was in geography with them. I've no reason to disbelieve them.'

Oriana put a hand to her forehead for a moment. 'All the same,' she said, 'I'd better go and check with Mavis. Meanwhile, you go to the staffroom and alert Max. Tell him Code Pink.' She caught my puzzled expression. 'That's St Bride's code to start the standard procedure to find a girl who has unaccountably missed a meal. Haven't you ever read your staff handbook, Gemma? Really, it's about time you did.'

I had tried several evenings in a row after I'd first joined the school, but after falling asleep over it every time, I'd put it to one side for when I would have more leisure and mental energy to focus on it. That time hadn't yet come, but now I regretted my omission. A missing girl, especially one identified as a high kidnap risk like Veronica, was potentially a serious problem. No one had seen her for at least an hour. She could be far away by now.

Oriana's further instructions made me fear the worst.

'Ask Max whether he's seen her anywhere or' – her voice cracked – 'whether he's seen any strangers on the premises – indoors or outdoors. I'll meet you back here in five. Don't worry about our tables, by the way. I'll put prefects in our places to supervise the rest of supper. We can eat later. When you've mobilised Max, give Rosemary a buzz and ask her to keep something hot for us, and also for Veronica when she turns up.'

I took comfort from her confidence that Veronica would reappear as soon as she was hungry.

To my relief, I reached Max on the staffroom phone at my first attempt. That meant I wouldn't have to track him down in any of his many hiding places.

'Hi, Max, it's me, Gemma. I'm so glad to have caught you in Rose Cottage.'

'In the nick of time. Just refuelled with supper ready for my first night patrol. Something wrong?'

I bit my lip.

'We've a girl missing from supper. You know what the girls are like, they never skip meals without good reason, but Veronica Thyssen has not turned up.'

'Have you checked with her housemistress that she's not sick?'

'Yep. Oriana's not seen her since lunch. Her classmates told me she was in her last lesson, geography, and Oriana's just gone to check whether Mavis noticed anything amiss.'

The line fell silent as Max took this in.

'Okay, Gemma, I'll do a high-speed recce of the grounds on my bike,

including all the outbuildings: mausoleum, gym, gardeners' hut. Get Joe
to check the sports pavilion and bike shed and to make sure no bikes are
missing. Easiest way to slip out at night is by bike. Pitch dark on the road
just now with this thick cloud tonight. I hope she has the sense to turn on
her lamps as soon as she hits the main road. Meanwhile, time for a fire
drill.'

'A fire drill? Surely that's the last thing we need right now. Can't it be
rescheduled for a less distracting time?'

'Textbook stuff, Gemma. First thing we do in the case of a missing
girl. Flush her out of hiding. Works like a charm.'

That made perfect sense. I retraced my steps to the small anteroom
from which the girls' meals were served, and where Oriana was waiting
for me, the faintest of lines now etched on her forehead, her lips pressed
together.

'Gemma, Mavis says Veronica was definitely in her last lesson. Didn't
say much, but that's Veronica for you. Next step: fire drill.'

'So Max said. I'd better go and get my fire drill register from the staff
room.'

'Okay, I'll alert Hairnet. But we'll only sound the alarm once the girls
have finished their desserts. Don't want them up half the night
complaining they're famished. We'll have enough chaos on our hands
just trying to find Veronica.'

As I sprinted down the corridor to the staffroom, I wondered at what
stage we should call the police. Presumably Hairnet would do that if
Veronica didn't appear for the fire drill. As I grabbed the fire register from
its usual resting place above the staff pigeonholes, I wondered how I was
meant to manage my Extra if a fire ever broke out in the staffroom.

19

FIRE DRILL

As soon as the girls began to file out of the Trough, I headed for the entrance hall and flipped the fire alarm switch that lay hidden behind an oil painting of the Reichenbach Falls. As the bursar had told me when first handing me the register, this bell was used only for fire practice. Unlike the various break-glass alarms dotted throughout the school buildings, this one was not patched through to the local fire station. However, the sound was indistinguishable from the real thing. All girls and staff treated it like a genuine emergency. Which, come to think of it, this time it really was, just not one involving fire.

Then I turned on the floodlights for the front of the house. We didn't want to compound our troubles by having anyone trip on the gravel and hurt themselves as they spilled out on to the forecourt to head for the muster station.

The girls swiftly organised themselves into ten rows of ten on the far side of the turning circle, the same groups that sat together at mealtimes. They all seemed to be enjoying the excitement of this unexpected interruption to their evening timetable, and none seemed remotely concerned that the building might actually be on fire. How trusting they were.

To simplify roll call, each group of girls lined up in alphabetical order by first name. Hairnet always listed the pupils by first name to show she valued girls as individuals rather than for their family names.

In front of each row stood the teacher that headed that group's table in the Trough. I had to stand at the centre of the turning circle with Hairnet and the bursar to co-ordinate the drill, so Rosemary took care of my girls. As each teacher completed their row's roll call, they sent the girl at the front of their line to report the results to me.

Did I say ten rows of ten? Make that nine rows of ten and one of nine, for conspicuous by her absence was Veronica, missing from the end of my table's row.

Abigail's eyes were mournful as she trotted over to officially report the bad news.

'We think Veronica's escaped. Do you think she posted herself home in her latest Harrods box? It's big enough, even for lanky old Vee.'

I wondered what other means of escape her friends had dreamed up.

'Thank you, Abigail, but I very much doubt it. A parcel weighing that much would be suspicious and the postman would discover her in no time and bring her straight back to school. Now return to your line, please.' The child was shivering in the damp night air. 'The sooner we get back into the warm, the better.'

Before I could confirm Veronica's absence to Hairnet, crunching gravel from the direction of the tradesmen's entrance made us all turn our heads. I doubted I was the only one whose spirits were lifted at the premature assumption that it was the errant Veronica returning, even though the long, steady sound did not resemble the footsteps of the slender twelve-year-old.

Instead, it was the noise of rubber tyres on gravel, the thick wheels of the ancient but efficient bicycle that Max sometimes used to patrol the grounds. He'd been cycling without lamps to give himself a stealth advantage. He didn't want Veronica to spot him from afar and flee, or indeed anyone else who was concealing themselves in the grounds. He dismounted, stood the bike on its prop, and came to stand in front of Hairnet, the bursar, and me. With rigid upright posture, arms straight at his sides, he looked as if he was about to salute to his military commander.

'No sign of the missing girl, Headmistress.'

From out of the shadows appeared McPhee, brushing against Hairnet's ankles. She scooped him up and wedged him close to her chest, stroking the top of his dark head with her free hand.

The bursar spoke in a low voice. 'Max, you do know Veronica Thyssen is a high kidnap risk, don't you?'

'Yes, sir.'

Hairnet narrowed her eyes at Max. 'Code Blue please, Max. Code Blue.'

This time, he really did salute.

Without wasting a second, Max climbed back on to his bike, kicked the prop back against the frame, and cycled out of the turning circle and across the pastureland. Droplets of muddy water flew up behind him on the tarmac, glinting beneath the floodlights, before the dark night cast its cloak of invisibility upon him.

I leaned towards Hairnet to speak in confidence.

'Hadn't we better call the police now?'

Hairnet shot me a sideways look that made me feel I'd overstepped my level of authority.

'Gemma, your job is done. You may stand down now. The bursar and I will take over from here, with the able assistance of Max. Your priority now is to reassure your girls that Veronica will soon be found safe and sound, and to curate a normal evening for them. You can tell them everything is in hand. They trust the adults here. That's all they need to know. Meanwhile, without asking direct questions that might unnerve them, listen in to their conversations and let me know if you hear any clues as to where Veronica might be hiding.'

Hiding? I wanted to say. A vulnerable twelve-year-old child, a high kidnap risk, had gone missing, yet Hairnet, Max and the bursar seemed to be treating her disappearance as a solo game of hide-and-seek.

The girls' chatter had been gradually growing in volume since the completion of the roll call. Hairnet clapped her hands three times to still their voices.

'Now, my dears, off you go to prep. I shall expect you to work extra

hard to compensate for missing the first ten minutes due to this routine drill.'

As everyone strolled back into the building, the girls were still speculating on Veronica's whereabouts. As Hairnet had requested, I eavesdropped without compunction as I followed my group through the entrance hall.

'Too busy playing with her latest Harrods haul, I expect.'

'I'm just disappointed that she didn't share it with us like she usually does.'

'Especially since she won all our pocket money in that stupid card game. Not to mention the IOUs.'

'We should call her Poker Face when she reappears.'

'I'd like to poke her face.'

In the stress of organising my first fire drill (and perplexed by why I'd never done one before – I made a mental note to ask the bursar for more frequent practice later), the IOUs had slipped my mind. Of course, that must have been the reason why the tuck shop takings had been so low. Veronica had left the girls with no cash to spend there.

Had she gone into hiding somewhere on the school estate because she was more scared of the girls' revenge than of fire? It seemed far more likely to me that as a high risk for kidnap, intruders had bundled her into a car under the cover of darkness, while everyone else, Max included, was enjoying their supper.

Looking up at the front of the house, I noticed all the windows had their curtains or shutters closed to preserve heat and save fuel. This would muffle any sound from outside, such as a kidnapper's car arriving and departing, even on this noisy gravel, especially if it was a near-silent electric vehicle. By now, Veronica could be miles away, with goodness knows who.

gambling that Max and Joe like to play to make them feel like bigger men.'

Despite my anxiety, I couldn't help but laugh.

'I'd never thought of it that way before. But you remember Max volunteered to teach the girls poker for essential life skills?'

Nicolette put her head in her hands. 'It seems he has taught Veronica too well. And her natural reserve gives her an advantage.'

I pictured the shy Veronica in my class, never as excitable or easily moved as her peers.

'Do you know the expression "poker face"?' I asked.

'*Ah, mais oui, le visage de poker!*'

She ran one hand over her smiling face, as if wiping her smile away, then stared at me, solemn now.

'The face that doesn't move?' she asked. 'The face that does not show what a person is thinking?'

'Exactly right. Don't you think it could have been coined for Veronica?'

'Coined?'

'Invented. Dreamed up. Inspired by.'

'So she has not allowed anyone else to win. That will not make her popular or please Hairnet. Ah, so I am right – the girls will have locked her in a cupboard to teach her a lesson. That is why she could not come to fire drill. Your theory is a good one, Gemma, better than a tale of the kidnap. What does Hairnet think of your discovery?'

Of course, that was what I needed to do next.

21

COLOURFUL THEORIES

There was an unwritten rule that no staff or girls could disturb Hairnet in her private apartment unless there was an emergency. Fortunately, as I dashed down the corridor from the staffroom to her quarters, I found her standing in the entrance hall, gazing out of the open front door. At the sound of my footsteps, she turned round to acknowledge me with a polite smile.

'Miss Harnett, please may I speak to you in confidence? I have something that may be relevant to Veronica's disappearance.'

'Temporary absence,' she corrected me.

After a final glance out into the darkness, she closed and bolted the door, then glanced at the wall clock.

'Let us repair to my study.'

In silence we marched down the corridor, not speaking until she was seated at her desk. I emptied the envelope of IOUs down on the clear space between her diary and her in-tray.

'Miss Harnett, I'm afraid I found these in Veronica's pigeonhole immediately before supper, before I realised she had disappeared.'

As she flicked through the pile of notes in silence, I began to explain.

'I think they're Veronica's winnings at poker. Presumably if the girls have had to resort to IOUs, she must already have cleaned them out of their pocket money.'

As Miss Harnett sifted through the notes, she pulled out a small, stamped envelope addressed in handwritten script to me. I slipped it into my pocket, not before noticing it bore a Cirencester postmark and was on Excelsior stationery. I must have scooped it up with the IOUs when I took them out of my pigeonhole earlier. I guessed it was a missive from Oliver, and if so, it meant he was still engaged in his local research. I'd assumed – hoped – he'd already returned to wherever it was he lived. London, according to his business card, unless he worked remotely from home elsewhere.

I determined to put Oliver out of my mind.

Hairnet patted the array of scrawled notes with a surprising show of satisfaction.

'Once Veronica is safely returned, I must make this a topic of an assembly. She can help me explain that one should only ever gamble what one can afford to lose. A useful life lesson.'

I must have looked perplexed because she went on to elaborate.

'You see, this term's essential life skills programme is not only about learning the rules of games. Any fool who can read instructions can learn to play a game. No, there are deeper lessons to be learned here, social and behavioural experience to be gained. Veronica is teaching the others that in spades, ha ha!'

How could she joke when one of her precious charges was missing? Perhaps her laughter was a smokescreen for her anxiety.

'But this one is no IOU letter,' she added, looking back at the pile of papers.

She pulled out another envelope that I had not noticed as it was plain white, like the notes, and unstamped. 'It is addressed to you, my dear.'

Handing it to me, she sat back expectantly. When she passed me the paperknife from her pencil pot, I realised she wanted me to open it and share it with her. I was glad she hadn't seemed interested in Oliver's letter, which I'd now hidden away.

The envelope bore my name in block capitals in multi-coloured ball-point pen, each letter a different shade – a favourite device of the girls to make the heading of an essay look more impressive. The paperknife, its point as sharp as a dagger, ripped through the flap as easily as a spoon parts sugar. I set it carefully back in the pot to avoid injuring myself before extracting the contents.

I pulled out a folded sheet of plain A4 printer paper and spread it out on top of the pile of IOUs. The message was painstakingly inscribed in the same rainbow capitals as the envelope. The correspondent seemed anxious to conceal their identity, rather than to win extra marks for presentation. Together we read it in silence.

I turned over the page to read the rest of the message, which in its entirety was rather long compared to the ransom notes I'd read about in crime stories:

RANSOME NOTE

IF YOU WANT TO SEE VERONICA THYSSEN ALIVE AGAIN, PLEASE MAY MISS LAMB DELIVER £247.62 TO DOILES TEA ROOM AT THE EXCHELSIA HOTEL IN CIRENSESTER AT 3 P.M. TOMORROW AND MR PIERS THYSSEN HAS GOT TO BE THERE TOO SO DON'T FORGET HIM OR ELSE YOU ARE IN BIG TROUBLE.

THANK YOU VERY MUCH AND BEST WISHES

'It looks like the work of one of the girls,' I said at last. 'At any rate, the handwriting looks immature, and the spelling leaves a lot to be desired.'

Hairnet gave a wry smile and there was a distinct twinkle in her eye.

'Oh yes, of course this missive has been written by Veronica herself, I've no doubt. That accounts for why her tricky surname is spelled correctly, but not the word ransom, or indeed Excelsior.'

She waved a hand to dismiss my concerns.

'It would also explain the insultingly low ransom figure,' she added. 'I suspect that amount suggested itself to her because it's the total of the money she's owed at poker.' She jabbed a fingernail at the figure. 'Thank you, Gemma, for bringing these notes to my attention. Now I must summon Max to update him. Meanwhile you may resume your normal duties until tomorrow afternoon, when I would like you to visit the Excelsior as instructed in this note to collect Veronica. I shall arrange cover for your lessons, and Max will accompany you at a discreet distance to reassure you you'll be safe. Not that I think you will be at any serious risk.'

Hairnet pulled an intercom out of her desk drawer to contact Max, asking him to report to her study immediately. By the time she returned it to the drawer, I had mustered the courage to challenge her judgement.

'But what of Veronica's safety in the meantime? Just because it looks as if she's written the note herself doesn't guarantee that she did or that she is safe. She might have written it under duress, at the instruction of an evil stranger. Or she might just have wandered off by herself into the cold, dark night. Even if she's not at risk from a stranger, she might succumb to hypothermia if she's out all night at this time of year. And if there really is a kidnapper, we don't know whether he will treat her kindly or harm her, Mr Thyssen or even Max. Or even if he—'

'—Or she,' put in Hairnet. 'Let's not be sexist here, my dear.'

'Either way, surely we have a duty of care to Veronica that means we can't just twiddle our thumbs waiting for 3 p.m. tomorrow to come around?'

I had a sudden flash of inspiration for how to motivate Hairnet to search for Veronica without further delay.

'Supposing the press got hold of the story? Where would that leave St Bride's reputation?'

Hairnet pressed her lips together in a thin line as she folded her hands on her desk.

'I will discuss the matter with Max directly, and if he concurs with my theory, we can all rest easy in our beds tonight.' Her eyes twinkled. 'And you may look forward to a hearty tea at Doilies tomorrow, at the school's expense.'

I was not so easily bought off.

'But how can either of you second-guess what her kidnapper is thinking?'

Resting one elbow on the desk, and her chin on her hand, Hairnet gazed at me defiantly.

'Because, my dear, Max was once a kidnapper himself.'

22

POACHER TURNED GAMEKEEPER

As Hairnet smiled in amusement at my stunned expression. I snapped my jaw shut, feeling foolish.

'You mean you think Max has kidnapped Veronica?'

She pushed back her chair, rose to her feet, and crossed to the antique mahogany sideboard to fill three dark-red crystal glasses of sherry from the matching decanter laid out on a gleaming silver tray.

'Dear me, no. If he had, he'd have had the sense to remove his IOU from the pile to conceal his possible motive. But he did used to be a kidnapper earlier in his career, when he learned a great deal about the way kidnappers and their victims and their would-be rescuers think. In fact, that is how I first became acquainted with him.'

I pictured Hairnet being held to ransom in a shady run-down villa, Max touching the point of a knife to her throat as he dictated his terms down the phone to whoever might pay good money for her safe return. Piers Galsworthy, perhaps? But that must have been at least thirty years ago, which would have been very early in Max's career.

'You mean Max is a poacher turned gamekeeper?'

She set a glass of sherry down in front of me, and another on the corner of the desk to await Max. From the third, she took a delicate sip.

'Something like that, yes.' Noticing my horrified expression, she laughed aloud. 'But that's all in the past now. Forgive and let live, my dear, is one of my mantras. It's never too late for a fresh start.'

Ha, she must have known that last remark might hit home, when St Bride's had given me the fresh start I needed in my life.

'Max is also a first-rate observer. Gemma, I can tell you no more just now, but please be reassured – and reassure the girls – that all shall be well. Now, drink your sherry – I think you need it – and be off with you. It's time for you to read the girls their bedtime story.'

She held up her hands and wiggled her fingers at me, but I was not so easily despatched.

'One thing's just occurred to me, Miss Harnett. Perhaps the ransom note is badly spelled because the person who wrote it is not a native English speaker.'

Hairnet's slender fingers toyed with the stem of her glass.

'Veronica is as English as they come,' she replied.

I shuffled forward on my chair, my hands on my knees.

'I know Veronica is, but she has a Bulgarian nanny and from what I've heard, she's a dubious character. One of Veronica's friends who went to stay with her last half term told me she'd been teaching them to swear in Bulgarian.'

Hairnet raised her eyebrows.

'How interesting! Perhaps they can teach me. On the essential life skills programme for a future term, we have useful words and phrases in a host of foreign languages. I hadn't considered Bulgarian until now. With Veronica's help, I can now add it to my list.'

She picked up her fountain pen, opened her daybook, and jotted a note for future reference. Then she looked up.

'Have you been watching too many old detective films, to make you assume that because someone is Bulgarian they must be a villain? Dear me, I would never have put you down for a xenophobe. Perhaps I should also add "embracing other cultures" to our essential life skills programme.'

I opened my mouth to protest my innocence, before realising she was right.

A sharp, rhythmic rap at the door heralded Max's arrival. When

Hairnet called, 'Come in!' and waved her hand to me, I realised I was dismissed. First, Joe and Oriana had shut me out, now Hairnet and Max. As I passed out of the room, Max entered and I left them talking in hushed whispers that only they could hear.

23

OLIVER'S LETTER

Although I wanted to believe Hairnet's conviction that Veronica was safe, I fleetingly considered calling the police myself. How would I sleep that night not knowing where she was? Despite her adult height and quiet air of self-assurance, she was a vulnerable, naïve twelve-year-old.

Shamefully I allowed Oliver's letter to distract me, at least temporarily, from Veronica's plight. As soon as I got back to the privacy of my flat, I retrieved the envelope from my pocket and ripped it open to extract a single sheet of cream hotel notepaper, covered in a staccato script on both sides. As a journalist, maybe he was more used to writing in shorthand for his own use than in longhand. I began to read.

Dear Gemma,

Please forgive me chasing you up, but I am at an impasse with my research. In the jigsaw puzzle of my father's biography, his service at St Bride's is the only missing piece. You will understand how even in the largest puzzle, the absence of that final piece can make the whole work feel meaningless and each of the other 999 pieces far less valuable. If I were religious, I'd liken it to the shepherd's grief for the lost lamb when the rest of his flock are safe.

Goodness, if this was representative of his prose style, how flowery would his finished book be? I realised he'd never told me what kind of publication employed him as a journalist. Perhaps a religious paper? Or maybe his emotions were just running high due to the nature of this private project. It continued...

I therefore beseech you

I didn't think I'd ever been beseeched before...

to do your utmost to extract from the school archives even the briefest detail of my father's time at St Bride's. I would be eternally grateful.

He was starting to sound like a character from a Victorian novel. I read on.

I remember from my own boarding school days how much I loved being in the company of other boys my age, some whom I came to regard as quasi-siblings. As an only child, I have no older siblings to remember my father on my behalf or to share their treasured memories with me. This feels like a great misfortune.

While keeping his enquiries a secret might protect the reputation of the school and Hairnet, was it really in Oriana's best interests to remain ignorant of her half-sibling, when she had only one other close relative, her mother? In her place, I'd have wanted to know about him. As an only child myself, I've missed out on the support of a brother or sister. Maybe if I'd had a sibling looking out for me, I would never have allowed my ex, Steven, to cause me so many problems.

The bell sounded for the younger girls' bedtime. Poor Oliver would have to wait.

I headed for the youngest girls' dorm, where instead of settling down in the armchair as usual to read the Year 7s their bedtime story, I sat on Veronica's empty bed. I hoped that filling her space would distract the girls from her absence. As I rearranged the items on her bedside table to direct the lamp on to my open copy of *Swallows and Amazons*, I lifted her money box, shaped like an old-fashioned treasure chest, expecting it to be weighed down by her accumulated cash winnings. But on finding an empty tin, my hand flew up in the air. Wherever Veronica had gone, she'd taken all her cash with her.

The girls didn't allow me time to consider. Having gained no intelligence about Veronica from Oriana during the leisure hour, they'd saved up their questions for me.

'Where's she gone?'

'Has she run away?'

'Who picked her up?'

'When's she coming back?'

'Is she hurt?'

'Is she safe?'

I set down the book and raised my hands for silence.

'Thank you, girls, for your generous care and concern, but you will please be assured that Miss Harnett and Mr Security have the matter in hand.' Oliver's old-fashioned turn of phrase was rubbing off on me. 'I am confident you'll be reunited with her soon. In the meantime, if any of you would like to speak to Miss Harnett about Veronica privately, Miss Harnett will be pleased to see you.'

As they fell silent, sliding down beneath their duvets, I opened our current bedtime story book at the marked page and began to read.

At the end of the chapter, I said goodnight, turned out their lights, and went to give the older girls their usual half-hour warning for their lights out, before heading back to my flat.

Just as I was closing my front door, I heard Oriana's open, and the sound of her speaking to someone in a low voice. When the person replied, I realised it was a woman, but no one that I recognised from the school community.

I couldn't make out what they were saying but could tell she had some kind of foreign accent. The only member of staff who sounded foreign was Nicolette, who retained a soft French burr in spite of her near-fluent English. This accent had a harder edge, but their voices were too muffled by the door for me to make out their exact words.

Veronica's Bulgarian nanny? Immediately I imagined Hairnet tutting at me and felt ashamed of my unconscious prejudice. Then their conversation stopped, and I could hear only the tapping of two sets of footsteps receding towards the stairs. A few minutes later, only one returned, followed by the click of Oriana locking her own front door for the night.

I slipped off my jacket and threw it on the coffee table before slumping on to the sofa and putting my feet up. As I did so, Oliver's letter fell out of my jacket pocket on to the floor. With so many questions about Veronica, Oriana, and Joe floating around my head, I decided to read the rest later and shoved it into my handbag, where it nestled beside the envelope that Judith had given me at morning break.

24

ON A MISSION

When I awoke the next morning, my first impression was of uneasiness, rising to acute anxiety, before I remembered the cause. Here was I, snug in my comfortable, cosy bed, my duvet held in place by a pretty violet silk counterpane, but where was Veronica? How had I managed an unbroken night's sleep without knowing she was safe?

I closed my eyes tight. I had put too great a faith in Hairnet's judgement and in the abilities of Max. Why was she so reluctant to call the police? For the sake of keeping the school out of the media?

To an extent I could see her point. The press would like nothing more than to spread rumours of the misfortunes of a private, fee-paying school; many journalists would jump at the chance to snaffle up stories of a posh kid gone astray. Those holes in the newspapers earlier in the term came to mind.

No matter how vigilant Max was at keeping out the odd intruder, once the mass media arrived at the gates in force, there'd be no chance of containing the story of a missing girl. Even if Max locked the big wrought-iron gates at the entrance to the drive, the press would find other ways in. I imagined them scaling the perimeter walls and fences, finding gaps in the hedge or using camera-bearing drones. An aerial view of the school would, like the board of Cluedo, provide the starting point for all sorts of conspiracy theories as to Veronica's disappearance.

Besides, it looked now as if Max had been unable to keep even one intruder out, because Veronica had disappeared in plain sight. She'd hardly have walked of her own accord into the arms of a waiting abductor. Even if she had 'kidnapped' herself, she must have had some sort of assistant to whisk her off the premises. If so, why hadn't Max spotted and stopped her co-conspirator? And what about Oriana's late-night visitor with the foreign accent? Might she be involved? Did Hairnet know about her? Was she playing it so cool about Veronica in order to conceal whatever her daughter was up to?

A shrill ring from the old-fashioned landline telephone on my desk jolted me out of my thoughts. I threw off the bedcovers, slid my bare feet into my slippers, and ran to see who it was.

Hairnet's voice was surprisingly calm. Had she slept as soundly as me? What was wrong with us both?

'Ah, Gemma, my dear, good morning.'

I rubbed my eyes as I returned her greeting.

'As we agreed last night,' she continued, 'I have arranged for you to accompany Max to Doilies this afternoon. You will need to miss the last two lessons, so please provide Oriana with some worksheets for your post-lunch classes so she may cover for you. I gather she owes you.' Her clipped tones told me she was not pleased with Oriana's recent bunking off to Cirencester.

'Say nothing to anyone about your planned absence,' she carried on. 'Oriana will tell the girls you are indisposed and allow them to believe you are resting in your room. When you reach The Excelsior, discreetly take a table in Doilies and stand guard there until you gain sight of Veronica. I believe she will be in the tearoom from 3 p.m. in the company of someone else whom you know only slightly. Keep out of their sight until they ask for their bill, then reveal yourself as if you've just met them by chance and offer to escort her back to school.'

I blinked. Accosting a kidnapper sounded a risky business, even if it was an acquaintance, as Hairnet suggested. I couldn't begin to guess who it might be. What made Hairnet think they would not put up a struggle, injuring either Veronica, Max, or myself?

Taking my stunned silence as consent, Hairnet continued.

'Neither condemn nor criticise her companion, nor the child. Just bring her straight to me on your return to school. I shall be waiting for you in my study.'

I swallowed. 'Am I expected to deliver the ransom money? Surely that's more in Max's line? Or as the note requests, should we instead be summoning her father to deliver the ransom?'

In the background I heard McPhee, probably curled up on Hairnet's lap, give a plaintive miaow. At least McPhee seemed to be rooting for me.

'No need for you to worry about the ransom money, my dear. I suspect it may not even be needed. But Max will be within shouting distance with the money in his pocket just in case my theory is wrong.'

'Your theory?' She had sounded so sure of herself that I'd started to assume she knew that Veronica was safe. Now it seemed she was just guessing.

I bit my lip and braced myself to challenge her. 'Have you alerted the police yet?' I pressed. 'I know they don't count adults as missing persons until they've been gone at least twenty-four hours, but surely for a child they'd want to know? And won't they want to arrest the abductor as soon as I've taken charge of Veronica?'

Surely Hairnet wasn't expecting me to make a citizen's arrest? I'd always wondered how those worked.

'No cause, no cause!' she cried. 'Now, there is the rising bell. Off you go for your morning duties, and remember, not a word to anyone about Veronica until you've returned her to me.'

That was easier said than done. It meant avoiding the staffroom and foregoing my coffee, to which, as I realised from my shaking hands, I'd become addicted.

After breakfast I returned to my flat on the pretext of having forgotten my bookbag, which I'd left there as an excuse. I lingered there until after the bell had rung for the start of morning lessons, so that all the girls and staff would already have set off for the classroom courtyard before I headed across. I didn't think I could walk alongside any of them without blurting out news of my secret mission or of my concerns for Veronica.

As I sat on my sofa, waiting for the bell for the first lesson, I itched to pick up my phone and dial 999. Why was I so hesitant? Like the girls, I trusted Hairnet. She had decades of experience, I told myself, and she loved the girls like her own. She knew better than me. She wouldn't take crazy risks. Would she?

Or was I just making excuses to avoid losing my job, knowing she had sacked my predecessor? Had living in this isolated artificial world, where her word and her whims were law, affected my judgement? Was I falling victim to some kind of brainwashing akin to Stockholm syndrome?

I'd just laid my hand on the telephone receiver to call the police when the school bell rang for the start of the first lesson. I jumped so much that I lost my balance, tumbling indecorously on to the floor and knocking my bookbag over, spilling its contents across the mauve rug. After scrabbling to gather them up, I raced for the door, conscious of Hairnet's aversion to lateness. By the time I reached my classroom and admitted the queue of shivering Year 7 girls waiting at the door, I was so puffed out and my heartrate so rapid that I told them to read quietly for five minutes, while I took slow, calming breaths, trying not to look at Veronica's empty desk.

25

OVER THE TOP

I wondered how to get through the day without mentioning Veronica. Even if I didn't raise the subject, surely the girls would ask me what was happening about her. Only at break did I discover that while I'd been lurking in my flat before the first lesson, Hairnet had called all the girls and staff into the hall for an impromptu assembly, and announced that Veronica would be returning after tea. No pressure on me, then.

She also told them not to waste time in idle gossip about her disappearance, but to welcome her back as if returning after a brief illness. No more should be said. Considering how much money the girls owed Veronica, that would take massive self-control.

The day's lessons couldn't go fast enough for me. Finally, at 2.30 p.m., after a quick cup of black coffee in lieu of Dutch courage, I jumped into my car and drove in quiet contemplation to Cirencester, following Max as his car turned right past the lodge houses and joined the main road.

The empty space in the hotel car park seemed a good omen for my strange mission, especially as it was right next to Max's car. I took comfort in his early arrival and tried to look relaxed as I marched up the front steps of The Excelsior's grand entrance, past the reception desk and into Doilies. The tearoom was almost empty, and I decided to head for a table in the far corner, where I could sit with my back to the wall and have a clear view of the whole room.

I panned the tearoom for Veronica, but she was nowhere to be seen. However, a familiar sight greeted me at a table halfway across the room: the back of the bursar's head, bent over a menu.

What was he doing here? Was he the person Hairnet had referred to as the one I knew slightly? Surely the bursar wouldn't be involved in kidnapping a pupil of St Bride's...? I braced myself to confront him.

When he looked up to give his order to the waitress, I realised it was not the bursar at all, but Oliver Galsworthy, ordering his afternoon tea. If he was trying to look like the bursar for some reason, he wasn't quite pulling it off. As Lord Peter Wimsey once said, 'Any fool can disguise his face, but it takes a genius to disguise a back.'

As the waitress departed and Oliver turned round to watch her go, I realised too late that I was sitting in his line of sight. A big grin lit up his face as he recognised me.

'Gemma, you came! How lovely to see you!' He motioned towards the empty chair opposite him, expecting me to sit down.

With the speed of a drowning man's life flashing before his eyes, I pictured Oliver kidnapping Veronica to extort information about his father, having given up on ever getting any results from me. But if so, why didn't he mention in the ransom note that it was documents he wanted, not that absurdly small sum of money?

I decided I had no option but to join him. I sat down.

'That would be lovely, Oliver, thank you.'

He raised his hand to recall the waitress and doubled his previous order, before leaning back in his chair to look at me quizzically.

'So, you did get my letter after all.' His tense shoulders dropped a little. 'I wasn't sure whether your school timetable would allow you to meet me this afternoon, but I'm very glad it did. I only have so much time I can spend here. I can't wait to see what you've brought me.'

What I'd brought him? What an odd thing to say.

'Did you find some of my father's photos? Or, what else have you been able to dig up? Honestly, when you didn't reply to my letter, after you sounded so keen to help when we met, I was about to give up on you.'

Suddenly in the distance, wearing a fluffy white bathrobe embroidered with the hotel's crest, Veronica flitted past the reception desk, hair dripping, mascara running down her heavily made-up cheeks. I guessed she was returning from the swimming pool and spa on the same floor of this sprawling hotel. Now, all alone, she was making for the lift, which I guessed meant she was heading for a hotel bedroom. Had her abductor realised she'd sneaked out for a swim? If her abductor was Oliver, unless he'd been able to lock the hotel door from the outside – not usually possible – she'd have been free to come and go while he was down here with me. If so, why hadn't she taken the opportunity to escape?

'So, let's see it then,' he persisted.

I reached into in my handbag and pulled out the plastic bank bag into which the bursar had carefully counted out the requested £247.62, and slid it across the table to him.

Puzzled, Oliver did a double take, and left it lying there.

'What's that for? What about the photographs? The press cuttings? The Speech Day programmes? Whatever else you could find about my father?'

'Oh, yes, I've got those too.'

I produced Judith's envelope, which by chance I hadn't taken out of my bag since collecting it from my pigeonhole, then picked up the little knife that lay next to my plate, cut the flap and spread the contents on the table in front of him.

26

THE UNEXPECTED

If Max was watching me from some hidden surveillance post, I wondered what he would make of the documents I'd just set before Oliver. Would Max realise who Oliver Galsworthy was? That Oriana had a half-brother? Perhaps Hairnet had confided in him for the sake of security. He knew Oriana was Hairnet's daughter, and he knew about Joe's troubled past. Would he know about Oliver too?

Oliver was busy perusing the documents, picking up each in turn to read intently, as if trying to memorise them in case someone might snatch them away. He held up a photograph of his father, Hairnet, and several other dignitaries on stage for Speech Day. Piers Galsworthy was standing at the lectern, facing the audience of parents and girls, his hands gripping the sides of the lectern as if he owned it. To his right, Miss Harnett was gazing at him uncritically, intent on whatever he might say.

'Can you see a family resemblance between my father and me?' Oliver was asking. He set down the photo, straightened his back, gripped the edge of the table and looked into the distance, imitating his father's stance.

I narrowed my eyes to focus on his chiselled jaw, his elegant broad shoulders, his neat hands – trying to identify similarities with the gentleman in the photograph.

'It's hard to tell when the original is so small. I suppose your hair colour is similar, though I can't really see the colour of Mr Galsworthy's eyes.'

He released his grip on the table, making the cups rattle slightly in their saucers.

'I'd always wondered if we were similar, because my mother never displayed my father's photos, so I'd never been able to compare myself directly to him. I suppose that must have been out of consideration for my stepfather's feelings. It would have been weird to have his wife's first husband watching over him. Once I began researching my father's biography, I also realised I didn't look much like him. That was disappointing.'

He scooped up the scattered sheets into a neat pile and tapped the side of the stack to align the edges.

'Please may I keep these?' he asked.

'Yes, they are for you. I had them photocopied especially.'

If Oliver was the kidnapper, he seemed remarkably calm. I needed to find out for sure. And if he wasn't, I should stop letting myself be distracted so that I could keep a lookout for the arrival of the real culprit. Anxious to get on with the purpose of my visit, I braced myself to move the conversation forward.

'So, I gather from your most recent note that you also had something to return to me?' I looked about me to check whether guests on other tables were listening in. I didn't want to mention Veronica by name.

Oliver paused, about to slip the papers into an old-fashioned leather briefcase that was leaning against his chair.

'Something to return to you? These documents are the first thing you've given me. What do you mean?'

'Well, when I say something, I actually mean somebody...'

I extracted the ransom note from my pocket, unfolded it and laid it out before him.

'You did send this to me, didn't you?' I pressed. 'If you didn't, I don't know who did.'

Oliver had just picked up the note, frowning, when a girlish squeal behind me made us both turn round to discover its cause. In the archway that led from the hotel reception to Doilies stood Veronica, who had just flung herself into the arms of a man – a tall, dark, lean man in a charcoal pinstriped business suit. His eyes were closed and a smile of unalloyed pleasure at their reunion played on his lips.

I'd only met him briefly a couple of times before, but I recognised Mr Thyssen at once as he hugged Veronica to him, oblivious of the wet hair that had left a dark trail down her back and was now dripping on to the cuffs of his expensive wool suit jacket.

'You came, you came! Daddy, you came!'

Veronica pulled back for a moment to gaze adoringly at her father, and he bent to kiss the top of her damp head.

'Yes, darling, here I am. Better late than never, eh? I'm all yours now for a wonderful afternoon tea. Let's try this famous chocolate cake, shall we?'

Veronica slipped her hand, with non-regulation scarlet-painted nails, into his, and with his free hand he summoned a waitress to show them to a table. She seated them on velvet banquettes in a booth within Oliver's field of vision, but just outside mine.

I slid down in my seat to avoid detection, as Hairnet had instructed. Besides. I didn't want to put a damper on this precious family moment.

'I wonder what's happened to our order for tea, Oliver?' I spoke quietly so that only he should hear. 'I could really do with a cup.'

Oliver gave me a funny look, as if he was starting to doubt my sanity, but politely humoured me by raising his hand to attract the waitress. As he did so, he inadvertently drew Veronica's attention, and the child leapt up from her seat to run across to me. Her eye fell on the bag of money on the table, and she reached out to grab it.

'Thanks, Miss Lamb, you're a real pal for bringing that,' she said, but she put it back on the table with a shy smile. Then with the good manners typical of St Bride's girls, she turned to acknowledge Oliver, offering her hand to shake. 'Hello, I'm Veronica Thyssen, and Miss Lamb is my English teacher. How do you two know each other?'

'Veronica!' called her father from across the room. 'I thought you wanted to spend some time with me? Come back, you little scamp, and eat your chocolate cake.'

He waved to me. 'Ah, Miss Lamb, isn't it? On your afternoon off? Please forgive my daughter for interrupting your date. I promise I'll deliver her back to school in time for supper.'

With a shower of chlorinated droplets flying from her hair, Veronica turned to skip back to her booth, and I slumped back in my seat.

'So you really were only after papers about your father?'

Oliver frowned. 'Yes, of course. Didn't you read the letter I sent you, inviting you to bring them here to tea this afternoon? I thought the offer of another of Doilies' famous teas would chivvy you along a bit. Why, what else did you think I was after?'

Now he mentioned it, I realised I'd been distracted from finishing reading his letter. The details of the invitation to tea must have been on the second page.

'It doesn't matter now,' I said quietly. 'As long as Veronica is safe.'

27

THE PRODIGAL PUPIL

It was almost suppertime when I returned to the school, driving alone in my car, with Veronica and Mr Thyssen following not far behind me in their Bentley. As it was dark, the bursar had already locked and bolted the front door, and I had to ring the bell to gain admission. By chance, Joe was the one to unbolt the door.

He would tell me later that he'd been half-expecting the caller to be a policeman, assuming that Miss Harnett had finally alerted the police to Veronica's disappearance, now that more than twenty-four hours had elapsed since she'd last been seen in school.

Like me, Joe had not been reassured by her insistence that all would be well. The previous evening, he'd been to see Hairnet after the fire drill to try to persuade her to call the police, brushing aside her concern to keep the school out of the newspapers.

He'd accused Hairnet of dereliction of her duty of care and had taken little comfort from her claim that Veronica hadn't really been kidnapped and that Max and I would soon bring her home safe and sound.

Then he'd offered to do a deal with Hairnet. If she would agree to call the police, then Joe would distract any scandal-seeking reporters that might turn up to investigate the story of the missing girl by revealing his true identity – giving them the scoop over national papers on a story of genuine public interest.

I was not surprised to hear she'd turned his generous offer down. It would just have been trading one damaging news story for another. After all, revealing the school had been harbouring a discredited athlete disguised as a woman might do just as much harm to the school's reputation as Veronica's disappearance.

She had also rejected as unnecessary his offer to accompany me and Max on our planned trip to Doilies to deliver the ransom money. I was touched and heartened that he'd volunteered. It made me realise he might still care about me after all.

With all his ideas quashed by Hairnet, he'd spent a sleepless night and an anxious day, feeling powerless to help, and fearing for my well-being as much as for Veronica's.

Now throwing the front door wide, Joe flung his arms around me with complete disregard for anyone who might witness our embrace.

'Oh my goodness, Gemma, I'm so relieved to see you safe home!'

As I collapsed into his arms, I realised how emotionally draining the last twenty-four hours had been.

'Oi! I'm the one who was kidnapped, you know!' came a high voice in the darkness behind me.

'Now, now, darling,' reproached a man's voice. 'I think that tale has run its course.'

Joe's grasp relaxed and we both turned to see Veronica and her father standing hand in hand, lit up by the motion-sensitive lamp beneath the portico.

Veronica, emboldened by her father's presence, pointed at me.

'No one kidnapped Miss Lamb, Miss Spryke. She was just having coffee in Doilies with some random man when I met Daddy there for tea. She was giving him photographs.'

Joe frowned at me in puzzlement. A range of scenarios must have been passing through his mind, but before he could ask any questions, a loud miaow behind us announced the arrival of McPhee, closely followed by Hairnet. McPhee trotted across to rub his cheek against my ankles, and Joe let go of me and took a step back for the sake of appearances.

Hairnet swept past us to take Veronica gently by the shoulders and kiss her on both cheeks.

'Veronica, my dear, I'm so glad to see you. Now, why don't you and your dear father step down to my study for a little chat. Thank you, Miss Lamb. You and Miss Spryke may go now.'

Mr Thyssen and Veronica stepped into the entrance hall and closed the door behind them, but before Joe and I could leave, Mr Thyssen reached out his hand to shake mine.

'Miss Lamb, may I just take this opportunity to thank you for taking such good care of my daughter? I'm sorry I didn't take the time to speak to you when I brought her back at the start of term, but Veronica has told me how kind you have been and how much she appreciates your care. That's why she chose you to receive her note. Thank you so much for understanding.'

I wasn't sure that I did, but an approving nod from Miss Harnett and the customary dismissive waggle of her fingers made me thank him politely and move to go. Before I could take a step, Veronica relinquished her grip on her father's hand and threw herself at me in a heartfelt hug.

'Thanks, Miss Lamb,' she said, her face pink with excitement. Perhaps embarrassed by this departure from her usual reticence, she swiftly disengaged herself and slipped her hand back into her father's. 'Sorry if I wrecked your date with your boyfriend.'

Fortunately, the supper bell rang, giving Joe and me the perfect excuse to turn away and march off towards the Trough without any further discussion. As we parted at the door to go to our respective dining tables, Joe leaned towards me and spoke in a low voice.

'Meet you in the staffroom straight after supper? I want to know everything that went on this afternoon, not least the identity of this supposed boyfriend...'

28

READING BETWEEN THE LINES

It was a huge relief to be able to tell the girls on my supper table that Veronica had returned safely to St Bride's, although I had to fend off questions about where she had been. Unsure what to reveal, I decided to leave it to Hairnet to agree a cover story with Veronica.

As it turned out, she was allowed to say she'd had a surprise visit from her father, who happened to be in the area on business spending the night at The Excelsior, and in her excitement to see him had neglected to seek permission from Hairnet before dashing off in a taxi to visit him. Hairnet made clear in a subsequent assembly that she'd forgiven Veronica for her oversight, because it was important for her to spend time with her father after he'd had to take his departure so suddenly at the start of term. But she also explained that it was absolutely a one-off, to guard against a barrage of similar requests from other girls.

It was even more of a relief to find Joe alone in the staffroom after supper. Now that it seemed we were still an item, I was longing to unburden myself about the situation with Oliver and his relationship to Hairnet and Oriana. I was desperate for his advice on how to handle the situation before I decided what to do next.

Solicitous for me in the aftermath of my ordeal, he settled me down on the biggest, comfiest sofa, lifted my feet on to the coffee table, and fetched me a cup of coffee before sinking down beside me for a debrief.

'I've been kicking myself for not defying Hairnet and jumping on my bike to follow you and Max to Cirencester,' Joe sighed.

He buried his face in his hands, shaking his head in remorse. When I patted his firm thigh to reassure him he splayed his fingers slightly and opened his eyes, staring ahead between the gaps.

'It's okay, Max was sent to shadow me. I wasn't on my own.'

'Even so, what were we thinking not calling the police last night, after the fire drill? I know Max scoured the grounds, and I checked the bike shed and sports pavilion, but it was such a dark night, and with no outdoor lighting beyond the school buildings, Veronica could have been lying injured or worse anywhere.'

'Blame Hairnet's leadership qualities. She was so convincing that Veronica would come to no lasting harm, we all believed her.' I took a sip of coffee. 'You know, it feels like such a safe little world here, it's hard to believe anyone could harm the girls. Every time we tell the parents or the girls how well we look after them, we convince ourselves a little more, to the point where we wouldn't allow ourselves to doubt Hairnet's words. Or at least not to act on our doubts. That makes us very vulnerable as well as the girls. Vulnerable to corruption, really. Plus of course we all want to hang on to our jobs and our sheltered, privileged positions in this educational Shangri-La.'

Joe sat back and ran his hands through his blonde curls.

'On the other hand,' he added, 'there's another possibility: that old Hairnet had inside information. She's the ultimate nurturer. I don't believe she'd genuinely put a single girl or member of staff at risk.'

I stared at him for a moment. 'You mean she knew it was a hoax and played along with it?'

Joe took the empty cup and saucer from my hands.

'Refill?' he asked.

I shook my head. 'No, thanks, I probably shouldn't even have had that one. My heart's still beating rather fast after all the excitement today, I'll never get to sleep tonight.'

I wrapped my arms around one of his and leaned my weary head on his shoulder. He wriggled to close the gap between us.

'So, this ransom note,' he began. 'How convincing was it? A child's prank or the work of a serious criminal?'

'It wasn't exactly convincing,' I admitted, 'The use of a multi-coloured pen to write each letter in a different colour did seem like the sort of thing a child would do. Pens like that are the kind you might find in their Christmas stocking. Plus the writer couldn't spell "ransom", which would be a bit of a rookie error for a professional kidnapper.'

'So how did they spell it? Like "handsome"?'

'Like the surname of the author, Arthur Ransome.'

As I said it, my hand shot to my mouth. 'How could I be so stupid? My junior dorm's current bedtime story is *Swallows and Amazons*.'

Joe threw back his head and laughed. 'By Arthur Ransome. Of course!'

I nodded.

'So somehow Veronica must have sneaked it into my pigeonhole during the afternoon,' I said. 'No, not even sneaked it. That wouldn't have been necessary. She could have just knocked on the door and asked any member of staff to put it in my pigeonhole. It was innocuous enough from the outside. All that was on the envelope was my name, in rainbow letters.'

A volley of taps at the staffroom door made us both crane our necks, as if x-ray vision would reveal who our caller was without having to get up from our comfortable seat.

Reluctantly, Joe detached himself from my embrace and ambled across to open the door. After he'd swung it open, he grinned at me over his shoulder.

'My word, Miss Lamb, I think we've summoned her up.' He turned back to speak to the visitor. 'Hello, Veronica, how lovely to see you.'

'Hello, Miss Spryke, and thank you very much, and lovely to see you too, but is Miss Lamb in the staffroom please? Miss Harnett would like to see her in her study please. I'm to go back there too.'

'Thank you, Veronica, she is. Please go and tell Miss Harnett that Miss

Lamb will be along in just a moment. There's something urgent she has to do first.'

'Okay, Miss Spryke.'

The patter of Veronica's feet told me she was skipping cheerfully back to deliver the message.

'Something urgent?' I lifted my feet from the coffee table. My legs had stiffened slightly in that position, and I stretched them before getting to my feet. 'Is there? What's that?'

Joe closed the door behind him and leaned back against it, both hands on the doorknob to keep out any more visitors.

'I want to find out who this "boyfriend" is that Veronica saw you having tea with.'

I sat back on the sofa, biting back a smile.

'You've no need to be jealous, Joe. That was no boyfriend. That was just a freelance writer, who wanted a bit of material about the history of St Bride's. I happened to be the only person on site when he turned up here last Sunday when you went out with Oriana, so I took the details of his enquiry and asked Judith to dig out some appropriate archive material. That's all.'

'Why didn't you put him on to the bursar? He's usually frontline for queries about the school's history and heritage.'

'Apparently, he'd tried that already and been ignored. The head too. The bursar completely ghosted him. He was very nice, and I felt sorry for him, so I thought I'd try to help. But there's much more to it than that. I'll tell you as soon as Hairnet's finished with me.'

Joe's taut shoulders relaxed. 'Okay, great. I'm sorry, I'm just being silly and inappropriately jealous.'

I bit my lip. 'To be honest, that wasn't the first time I'd had tea with Oliver at Doilies. He took me out on Sunday too. This was a second fixture, so to speak. It was probably a bit rash of me to go off with him that day, but, well, you'd gone off with Oriana, so...'

I fizzled out, realising this risked making things worse rather than better. First I needed to explain that I only went on that first date to protect the school's reputation – and Hairnet's. Why did everything have to be so complicated?

Joe coughed. 'Ah yes, and in return I must tell you more about my recent outings with Oriana. There's a very good reason for those which I'll be more than pleased to tell you now everything has been resolved.'

But before we could enlighten each other and be truly reconciled, another volley of knocks landed on the staffroom door, and Joe swung round to open it.

'Miss Spryke, Miss Harnett told me to ask you whether you've kidnapped Miss Lamb?' Veronica broke into peals of laughter.

Joe's alibi would have to wait. I hastened to Hairnet's study before I could get into any more trouble.

29

A STUDY IN PARENTHOOD

Veronica trotted over to the sofa on which her father was sitting primly, balancing a cup of tea on his lap. Although there was plenty of space on the sofa, Veronica sat right beside him, touching her father from shoulder to toe.

'Please take a seat, my dear,' said Hairnet to me gently, pointing to the sofa opposite Mr Thyssen and his daughter. 'I know you are fond of stories, and I would like Veronica to share with you the fascinating tale she has just told me. But the abridged version please, Veronica. I think we have spent almost enough time on it now.'

Veronica sat up and looked me straight in the eye.

'I'm very sorry, Miss Lamb, it's all my fault.'

With a meaningful glance at me, her father touched her arm in restraint, an admission of his share in the blame. But Veronica continued.

'I wanted Daddy to make up for the afternoon tea he missed at Doilies at the start of term, so when I won all that money at poker, I thought I'd treat him, in case the real problem was that he didn't have enough money for it. You see, he'd been complaining all the way back in the car about the school fees.'

Mr Thyssen coughed and lowered his eyes. 'Sorry, Miss Harnett.'

Miss Harnett accepted his apology with a wave of her hand.

'I was going to ask him to pick me up from school the next afternoon but then I saw a taxi without anyone in it by the portico straight after geography. I had a brainwave. I asked the taxi driver to wait for me while I wrote a note and put it in your pigeonhole, then grabbed some things from my dorm, and they drove me to The Excelsior.'

I frowned. 'How come a taxi was just standing there doing nothing?'

'It had dropped a visitor off for Miss Bliss – some foreign lady. The taxi driver said she came from Oz. Is that a real country? I thought it was a made-up one, that green place in The Wizard of Oz.'

'You mean the Emerald City?'

She nodded, happy to accept Frank L. Baum's story as a documentary.

'Anyhow, the lady wasn't going back to Cirencester until later in the evening, so the taxi was free.'

'Why go to The Excelsior the night before your father was coming to tea?'

'I could afford it after all the money I won at poker. Mr Security is such a good teacher. I think you should let him teach us other lessons too. Besides, I thought, if Doilies' cakes are so delicious, so must their breakfasts be, and I bet their beds are super-comfy too. Unlike my bed in my dorm.' She shot a look at Hairnet, who picked up her pen to make a note in her diary.

'I will speak to the bursar about it,' she murmured. 'We do have a few spares in the cellar we might swap it with.'

'So, anyway, I booked a room, and it was a very nice room too.'

I turned to Hairnet. 'The Excelsior let a lone child book a room? That's inexcusable.'

Veronica folded her arms across her chest. 'I turned twelve on Boxing Day. Besides I was wearing some of the make-up I got in my last Harrods box, so I looked more grown-up. Anyway, I'm as tall as some grown-ups too.'

'So had you told your father at this point what you'd done?' I asked, turning to Mr Thyssen who was fiddling with his teaspoon.

'I'm sorry, Miss Lamb, I had no idea, or I'd have told her to go straight back to school. I knew nothing of her fanciful plot until Miss Harnett kindly telephoned last evening to request my presence at Doilies at 3 p.m. today.'

'Just after the fire drill,' I said without thinking. 'So you knew where Veronica was all along?'

Hairnet's smile bore a trace of self-satisfaction.

'Of course. Surely you didn't think I would let one of my young charges wander unchecked?'

At that moment I wasn't quite sure what to think.

'The manager of the hotel phoned me as soon as Veronica arrived,' Hairnet carried on. 'In the meantime, Max had alerted the police. I told him Code Blue, remember?'

'Ah, Code Blue! So that's what that means.'

When Hairnet tutted, I realised how remiss I'd been in not yet reading the staff handbook and was grateful she didn't think it appropriate to tell me off in front of Veronica and her father.

She continued. 'You see, Mr Thyssen, we use these codes in school so as not to panic the girls. It is never a good idea to make a drama out of a crisis. So the hotel manager – a trusted friend of our housekeeper Gerry, I might add – sought my instructions, which were to take the best care of her until her father arrived for tea the next day. As I knew he would, once I had explained to him how important it was to Veronica to see her father there. The ransom note you showed me made everything fall into place.'

Veronica clasped her father's hand, making his teacup wobble perilously. He set down his cup and saucer to take both of her hands in his.

'I promise next time your friends arrange a tea party with their parents there, I shall make the time to attend,' Mr Thyssen said earnestly.

'So all's well that ends well,' Hairnet concluded.

She laid down her pen, closed her diary, and clasped her hands on top of her orderly desk.

Mr Thyssen coughed. 'Now I'd better be getting back up to town.' As he stood up, he held out his arms to his daughter.

Veronica fell into his embrace, eyes shut tight with pleasure. Without letting her go, her father spoke to us above her head.

'Thank you, Miss Harnett, Miss Lamb. I cannot thank you enough for taking the time to understand and support my daughter. I'm sorry if I have seemed a little remiss in that regard. The pressures of work, you know, especially after the break for the Christmas holidays.'

Veronica extracted herself from her father's arms and they both sat back on the sofa, bodies nestled against each other like a father bird caring for its fledgling.

'But it won't be a problem any more, will it, Daddy? Because now you'll have someone else to look after you in term time when I'm not there.'

'Your nanny?' I queried, puzzled.

'No, Sharon. Sharon's moving in with us.'

'Your PA?' A live-in PA was surely the sign of a workaholic. Perhaps he hadn't learned his lesson about taking more time off to spend with Veronica after all.

A slight smile played around Mr Thyssen's lips.

'My former PA. And my future wife. As I told Veronica over tea this afternoon, I've asked Sharon to marry me, and she said yes.'

'Which is why this week's Harrods box was so good,' put in his daughter. 'Sharon got to know me better over Christmas, because she spent it at our house, and now she knows just the sort of thing I like. Although I did tell her she'd better stop sending these boxes and save the money to spend on the wedding instead. Besides, I want to make sure they've got enough money to get me a decent bridesmaid's dress. So, she said she'd send me one last one, with all the make-up and stuff I was interested in.'

Miss Harnett smiled her approval. 'How very selfless of you, my dear. Although you know my feelings about make-up. Not to be worn in school, if you please.'

Veronica shrugged. 'That's fine by me.'

'And no more poker, either, Veronica,' Miss Harnett added, 'not for money, anyway, and only then if you allow the others to win sometimes.'

'To be honest, Miss Harnett, I don't care if I never play that silly game ever again. I didn't like taking my friends' money. It was awful seeing the sad looks on their faces as they slid their cash across the table to me. That's not how winning should feel.'

As Mr Thyssen got to his feet, he gave a little smile of pride in his daughter's generous attitude.

'Now I really must go,' he said. 'But I stand corrected. St Bride's School fees really are worth every penny. Thank you again for alerting me last night to Veronica's needs.'

'I'll walk you to your car,' said Veronica, slipping her hand into his, and Hairnet and I sat in silent contemplation until their footfall faded at the far end of the corridor.

30

THE CHILD SPARED

For a moment, Hairnet and I gazed at each other. I was unsure whether to laugh or cry. Seeing Veronica basking in her father's affection had been a delight, but at the cost of considerable anxiety and trouble to us all. Or to me, anyway. Hairnet seemed rather gleeful about the whole issue.

'So, what will her punishment be?' I asked at last.

Miss Harnett tutted as she rose to fetch us each a glass of sherry from the cabinet under the window.

'Punishment? Why on earth should I punish her? I think the poor child has suffered enough, being emotionally neglected by her father in front of all her friends. I just hope this Sharon is all that Veronica is hoping for. If she softens Mr Thyssen up a little, so much the better. There's a gentler soul inside that stiff exterior, trying to get out, if only he could forget his wretched business concerns for long enough to spend time on what really matters.'

I took my sherry glass from her. The Venetian glass sparkled like a ruby.

'From what Veronica's told me, it sounds as if he's been grieving for his late wife the whole of his daughter's life. He doesn't allow photos of her or of them as a family around the house. Veronica needs to see these photos, surely?'

Hairnet held her sherry up to her desk lamp to admire the amber liquid, which had turned the colour of mahogany when viewed through the dark-red glass.

'Perhaps Veronica reminds her too much of his late wife as she grows up. That must be hard for a man.'

'But surely it might also be life-affirming to see his late wife live on through their daughter?'

She set her glass down in the pool of light beneath her swan-necked bronze desk lamp.

'Quite so, my dear, quite so.'

The slight crack in her voice made me realise I might have touched a nerve. How much did Oriana resemble her father? Was that why Hairnet tolerated her constant image changes, because it made her less like her late father?

'So, there is to be no punishment, Gemma. Veronica will not reoffend.'

The sherry, sending a warm glow through my veins, gave me the confidence to speak my mind.

'But the hotel? Surely you will reprimand the Excelsior for letting a room to a lone minor?'

She picked up her fountain pen and ran a fingertip over the raised floral pattern around the rim of the cap.

'Quite the contrary. They managed admirably. The staff humoured her by checking her in on arrival. She paid cash, you know, all in coins. They thought she would be safer if allowed to stay than if they turned her away. They guessed she was one of our pupils, despite the make-up she'd applied in the hope of passing for an adult. No cosmetics could disguise that little-girl voice, nor her propensity to skip rather than walk down the corridors. The duty manager called me immediately after she'd checked in and emailed me a still from their security cameras to confirm her identity. She had checked in under the name of Susan Walker, you know. Such a giveaway. No-one of her generation is called Susan these days.'

'Susan Walker? That's the name of one of the children in *Swallows and Amazons*!'

Hairnet smiled as she reached for the bottle of green ink beside her lamp, unscrewed the barrel of her pen and proceeded to refill it.

'Exactly. Of course, I could have sent Max to pick her up and bring her back to school straight away, but I thought it better to let her get it out of her system. Spending a night alone in the hotel would soon have her missing her friends in her dormitory.

'Besides, the Excelsior struggles enough to stay in business, as does any country hotel in this age of budget motels cloned up and down the country. When they'd done the decent thing, I didn't like to rob them of a respectable paying customer.

'I asked the manager not to let her leave the hotel until her father arrived the next day, and to get a female member of staff to check in on her every once in a while. She'd be well fed. She's stayed in enough hotels in her life to know how to use room service and how to put restaurant meals on her room bill.'

'I suppose she had plenty of cash on her anyway,' I put in, 'with all the money she'd won from her friends at poker. Is Max in trouble for letting her fleece them all?'

She screwed the lid tightly on to the ink bottle and returned it to its place by the lamp.

'Ah, Max. Veronica told me she thought Max was letting her win to build up her confidence as a player. But he says she's just a natural. Her poker face will be extremely useful, whatever she goes on to make of her life.' She uncapped her pen, flipped open her daybook, and began to write. 'I am putting her down for a new award at Speech Day: Most Inscrutable.'

Hairnet made a point of finding an admirable quality or achievement to recognise in every girl each Speech Day.

'But I have explained to her that gambling should be enjoyed only in moderation, or preferably not at all. Avarice was not her motivation, and she has offered to cancel all those IOUs and to refund the money won from her friends. All she really wanted was to see her father.

'I shall also arrange for a future essential life skills course in spotting, treating and avoiding addictive behaviour. Although that won't be in the same term as they are taught how to place a bet on the Grand National and how to mix and serve cocktails – all theory at this stage, of course, due to their young age. I believe in moderation in all things, my dear, including moderation.'

I guessed she wouldn't be offering me a second helping of her delicious sherry.

Finishing my drink, I got up to return my empty glass to the silver salver on the cabinet before bidding Hairnet goodnight.

'One thing I still don't understand, Miss Harnett. That ransom note. What was the point of that? And why the strange value?'

Hairnet smiled. 'A paltry sum for anyone's daughter. She only chose that amount because it was front of mind as the total of the IOU debts. I gather she didn't really want the ransom money and that you still have it.' I realised I did. 'I suppose she thought presenting her disappearance as a kidnap would make it more likely that her other demand – to see her father – would be met. Girls have such vivid imaginations at her age. Fiction can seem as real as fact.'

I smiled. 'Perhaps next term I'd better find a less adventurous bedtime story than *Swallows and Amazons*.'

31

RECLAIMING JOE

Back in my flat, and realising how lucky I was that this escapade had ended without anyone being harmed, I began to wonder: how could I have lived with myself knowing that I hadn't defied Hairnet's directions and notified the police when I'd thought it a real emergency? Had any of my colleagues done so, or were they, like me, too fearful of losing their jobs to cross her? As I began to get ready for bed, I vowed I'd never be so cowardly again.

One might have thought that after the safe resolution of Veronica's disappearance, I would have slept soundly in my secure, cosy flat. Instead, I spent a sleepless night, imagining alternative endings: a real, vicious kidnapper murdering Veronica; an intruder attacking her in her hotel room; Mr Thyssen refusing ever to leave his world of work to reclaim his daughter. Even Mr Thyssen's planned remarriage morphed into a threat in my sleep-starved brain, the latest Harrods box part of a plot to lure Veronica into mistaking Sharon for an ally before she ousted the child completely from her father's affections.

So after breakfast the next morning, my resistance was low when Joe buttonholed me to invite me to afternoon tea at Hector's House. He said he wanted to share what he'd been going to tell me the previous night, before I'd been summoned to the head's study, and I welcomed the opportunity to confide in him about Oliver and Oriana too. It wasn't our afternoon off, but we both had free periods, giving us just enough time to drive the round trip to Wendlebury Barrow and have twenty minutes for our tea.

* * *

'Your usual, folks?'

As ever, Sophie's friendly welcome immediately put me at my ease. Hector, engrossed in typing something on his laptop, acknowledged us with a cheery greeting on our arrival, but didn't seem to be listening to our conversation.

Sophie unloaded a tray of tea things on to our table before excusing herself.

'I'm just nipping out to the stock room to unpack some deliveries and add them to our inventory. If you need me, just come and bash on the door.'

Much as we usually enjoyed Sophie's company, this time we'd be glad of some privacy.

'It's good to get out with you at last,' Joe began.

I concentrated on pouring our tea.

'Gemma, I've been wanting to tell you why I've been spending so much time with Oriana lately, which I recognise has been at your expense or rather at a cost to our relationship, and I'm sorry. But now at last I can tell you everything, and believe me, it's all good news.'

I sliced my scone with surgical precision, then spread a blob of clotted cream on top, paying as much attention to its evenness as a plasterer to a wall.

'My outings with Oriana weren't dates, if that's what you were wondering.'

My knife slipped, slicing a deep channel through the thick layer of cream. I repaired it before adding a teaspoon of gleaming strawberry jam, my hopes mounting.

'But here's one thing you won't have guessed,' Joe continued. 'Together we've been meeting my ex-girlfriend, Eleonora Simpson.'

I hadn't seen that coming. My knife clattered to the floor, and I bent to retrieve it, pretending to search for far longer than I needed to, while I digested this surprising piece of news.

When I sat up again, Joe was drinking his tea, gazing at me anxiously over the rim of the cup. I laid my dirty knife on the edge of my plate.

'I thought this was meant to be good news? I don't suppose Oriana enjoyed playing gooseberry.'

He reached across the table to take my hands.

'Sorry, Gemma, I'm making a right mess of this. Let me start again.'

I pulled my hands free on the pretext of wanting to drink my tea. I held the cup to my lips without drinking for a moment, letting the rising steam warm my cheeks before I took a comforting sip.

'Remember Edward Simpson?' Joe asked.

I put down the cup and began to fiddle with my scone, pushing a loose sultana back into the dough.

'How could I forget him?'

I'd never met him, but without his betrayal of Joe, I'd never have met Joe either, so I felt a strange blend of anger and gratitude towards Edward.

'The thing is, his sister, Eleonora, got back in touch with Oriana over the Christmas holidays. She and her brother went to live in Australia a couple of years ago and they both took citizenship to start afresh. They've even acquired Australian accents to help them blend in, as they're planning to stay there long-term. As you know, Oriana was Eleonora's friend before she knew me – they'd met a decade before at teacher training college – and although she was disgusted at the way Eleonora and Edward treated me, she and Eleonora kept in touch.

'At Christmas, Eleonora confided in Oriana that her brother had stupidly squandered all the money he'd made from selling his story to the press, and between them they'd devised a rescue plan. He was to announce a follow-up to his original story, saying that his wilderness years had led to an epiphany. Now he wanted to be completely open about the matter so that others might learn from his mistakes. Eleonora had engineered a book deal for him, signed him up for public speaking coaching, and got him taken on by an agency for inspirational after-dinner speakers.'

I folded my arms and sat back in my chair. As I crossed my ankles, I touched Joe's foot by accident and let it stay there.

'So how does that help you? Surely it'll just get your name dragged through the press again?'

'Yes, but this time in a positive way. You see, Edward's new book completely exonerates me. Not like the half-truths and half-lies he told to the press before.'

'But how can it? I'm sorry Joe, but you did wrong, letting him substitute your urine sample for his own, for the sake of keeping in with his sister.'

Joes passed his hand over his mouth. 'Actually, I didn't do that at all. We'd both been asked to give random samples on the same day, while I was staying at the flat he shared with his sister. Edward and I went down to the lab together, and I was dreading his being rumbled. But I needn't have worried. Somehow, in an example of extraordinary oversight by the monitoring company, Eleanora had wangled a job as a temporary clerk checking in the samples and passing them on to the lab technicians for testing.

'Although Edward knew this – in fact, it had been his idea that she should apply when he read on his previous visit that there was a vacancy in admin – I had no idea until she told me much later. Working on her own in a little office, it was ridiculously easy to discard Edward's original sample, substitute a new bottle and decant into it part of the contents of mine. I would never have agreed to such fraud, of course.'

'So you've been covering for her as much as for him all this time? You told me you'd been persuaded to help Edward cheat.' I took a bite of scone and chewed slowly to buy thinking time. 'So do you still have feelings for her?'

Joe gazed into the distance for a moment.

'I suppose I did when it happened, then for a while afterwards. I felt a duty of care towards her. It was a serious relationship. We'd been seeing each other for a couple of years, and that's too big an investment of time to throw away lightly. But honestly, Gemma, when I met her again in

Cirencester with Oriana on Sunday, I couldn't understand what I ever saw in her.'

I helped myself to Joe's knife to cut my scone into bite-sized pieces.

'So she is finally coming clean about what she did too?'

'Ha! Funny you should say that, Gemma, because that's the title of his book: *Coming Clean*. Yes, the two of them take all the flak, and I emerge as the good guy.'

I considered this for a moment. 'Are you sure? Have you read it?'

'Yes, and so has Oriana's lawyer friend. The lawyer came to see Oriana last night after supper to go through all the details and to give Oriana advice for me.'

'Ah, the lady who arrived in the taxi that later took Veronica to Doilies.'

'So it seems. She counselled me to resume my proper identity now that my name is to be cleared and to stop living this silly double life. I can't pretend that wouldn't be a huge relief.'

I tried to smile. 'You might have told me, Joe. It would have saved me an awful lot of worry.'

Joe had the decency to look ashamed.

'I'm sorry, Gemma, I know I could have trusted you. But Oriana insisted on keeping it completely hush-hush. She was so worried about something leaking out to the papers and causing a scandal for St Bride's.'

I could understand that. It couldn't have been easy for either of them. I wanted to make him feel better, but there was one thing still worrying me.

'I'm happy for you, but I assume that means you'll have to leave St Bride's?'

He scratched his head. 'I don't know. Oriana's going to speak to her mother about it and see what she thinks. It would take a lot for her to change her mind about allowing male teachers at St Bride's after all this time, because it would look as if we've abandoned one of our basic principles. Any fathers who chose the school for its single-sex ethos might simply remove their daughters from the school. Goodness knows, the school is close enough to the brink already without risking losing pupils through a sudden policy change. It would also be expensive in practical terms: she'd have to reprint the prospectus, revise the website, and so on. All this, and we still haven't dealt with the fact of the lie itself, which in itself could harm St Bride's reputation...'

'But your choice would be to stay?'

He nodded. 'Of course. No teacher ever leaves St Bride's unless forced out, like Katie Donovan. It's far too cosy a niche, and the beautiful setting spoils you for anywhere else.' He put his head on one side, his eyes twinkling. 'As do my colleagues, one of them far more than the rest.'

Suddenly realising how hungry I was, I put the biggest piece of scone in my mouth – the thick cream, slithery jam and crumbly dough a delicious combination of tastes and textures.

He watched me in silence until I'd finished my mouthful.

'Well, if Oriana can't persuade Hairnet to let you morph into Mr Spryke somehow, no one can, although it's not going to be easy to explain it to the girls,' I said at last. 'But if the story's going to be all over the press, I could understand if she said no. By the way, are you sure it hasn't already been in the papers? Maybe that's what those missing newspaper articles were about: your troubled past.'

Joe reclaimed his knife to slice his own scone.

'No, I'm sure it wasn't,' he said. 'The book's not out until July, and Edward's publisher has embargoed all information about it until March, when they plan to launch a big publicity campaign. Edward isn't daft enough to spoil his comeback by leaking details in advance.'

I bit my lip. 'March, eh? That doesn't leave us long to persuade Hairnet to keep you on.'

'I'm glad you said "us", Gemma. But what do you really think? At the moment, you've got as good a poker face as Veronica's.'

I reached for his hands and gazed into his eyes.

'I'm with you every step of the way, Joe, if you want me.'

Just then, a scruffy old man came across to sit at the next table, pausing on his way past to wink at us. It was Billy, a regular at the tearoom and the pub across the road too.

'Oi, it's not even Valentine's Day yet!' he cried, wagging a forefinger.

'Oh, let them be, Billy,' said Sophie, emerging from the stockroom.

She marched back to the tearoom counter to wash her hands at the basin. 'It's never too early to warm up for Valentine's Day, is it Hector?'

Hector looked up from his keyboard and winked at her.

'I'm game if you are, sweetheart.'

Joe glanced at his sports watch.

'Speaking of time, we'd better hurry up and finish our tea, Gemma. We'd better not be late for our next lesson if we want to keep Hairnet onside.'

32

PERSUADING MISS HARNETT

Oriana waited until the weekend to choose the best moment to tackle her mother about Joe's proposition.

'You'd think she'd have noticed that no other girls' school in this day and age have a "women only" staff policy,' she said, as we strolled round the lake together after Sunday lunch, making the most of the sudden clearing of the wintry skies. The sun was so bright that I wished I'd brought my sunglasses. Whenever the water was disturbed by passing ducks, ripples sparkled like tinsel.

'Oh, but she doesn't really, Oriana. There's not only Max and the bursar and Gerry, but all her governors are men, haven't you noticed?'

Oriana stooped to pick up a leaf skeleton the colour of cinnamon and held it up to examine the complex structure of its ribs against the pale sunlight.

'Yes, but only because she generally recruits the fathers of past girls as governors, hoping they'll leave legacies to school funds when they pop their clogs. That's how the most recent refurbishment of the dorms was paid for. There's no room for anything beyond basic maintenance and troubleshooting from fee income, not with such a small school roll.'

I watched a duck turn up its tail to search for food below the surface, holding my breath until it resurfaced.

'Didn't Kate Barker used to be a governor? You know, the lady from the village – Hector's godmother?'

Oriana held the leaf skeleton at arm's length and let it go. We stopped walking to watch it float slowly down and land in the lake like a tiny ghostly boat.

'Yes, when she volunteered to be a governor, Hairnet didn't like to say no. Good on Kate, I think she was hoping to reform the system from within. But she didn't last long. All these old men must have given her the creeps. Their board meetings are like a visit to God's waiting room. Kate still does stuff for the school sometimes. She donated our peacocks, you know. Such a pity the old boys drove her away. She was a breath of fresh air.'

I was sorry for Hairnet too that the governors had driven Kate away. Hairnet must have been glad of her presence as another strong woman.

'So, Gemma, I'm going to suggest she calls a special governors' meeting to review the issue of male staff. I'm hoping Veronica's little drama will sway them in our favour, because wasn't that whole business the perfect example of a child needing a male role model? And if the girls' fathers are sending them away to school for weeks at a time, all the more reason to field a substitute in term-time.'

Oriana's voice cracked slightly, and when I glanced at her out of the corner of my eye to assess why, her cheeks were flushed and her eyes were shining with unshed tears.

'It must be...' I was about to sympathise with her own position as a lifelong fatherless child, but something stopped me. I tried again. 'It must be especially hard for the girls who didn't have brothers at home to spend time with in the school holidays, or even sisters.'

As we rounded the far end of the lake, Oriana bit her lower lip to hold back the tears, and I realised how lonely she was herself for a sibling of some kind. I resolved to introduce her to Oliver when I could. Better to have to seek Hairnet's forgiveness afterwards than to ask her permission and risk a refusal.

I cast around for a diversion.

'Oh, Oriana, just look at all these beautiful cyclamen!' A splash of scarlet basked in the direct rays of the sun beside a stone garden seat.

'Seeing the odd burst of colour like that makes you realise spring is on its way.'

'Yes.' She forced a smile and we continued our circuit of the lake in companionable silence, broken only by the hoarse quacks of ducks.

33

JOE'S SECRET

Joe saved his news for our next shared afternoon off.

'I've something to celebrate.'

That much was apparent from his radiant smile as he met me in the corridor outside my flat after the bell had rung for afternoon lessons. 'Shall we splash out and go to Doilies for our tea at the weekend? If so, bring your car keys. You won't want to cycle all the way to Cirencester in this windy weather.'

I grimaced. 'You're right there. Maybe next term if the weather is better. But I'm happy to go for a drive. Perhaps we'll spot some early lambs along the way. I love seeing new-born lambs in the spring.'

He laughed.

'It would be odd if you didn't, Miss Lamb.'

As we strolled down the marble staircase, Joe was almost bouncing with excitement, but I guessed his news would have to wait until we were off the premises, so as not to be overheard by any girls.

'Where are we most likely to find lambs?' I wondered aloud as we drove between the gatehouses.

'Let's get away from the main roads where it's quieter. Take a right, then a left, and we'll amble along the minor lanes.'

The heavy morning frost had long since melted, but the sunshine on this crisp, still day had not been hot enough to burn off the watery residue, and the short damp grass was sparkling. Before long, we passed a couple of fields where we were delighted to find a few tiny lambs were shadowing their mothers, gambolling extra steps to catch up whenever they moved on.

'There's a lay-by just coming up on the left,' said Joe. 'Let's pull over and walk back to get a better look.'

Once parked, we strolled hand in hand along the broad grass verge towards the field full of chunky, solid ewes, their fleeces dark as January clouds looming over their cotton-wool-white new lambs.

Side by side, we leaned on the wooden five-bar gate at the corner of the field, moving slowly and quietly so as not to spook the sheep and make them run away. I stood on the lower rail and leaned over the top bar to pick off a clump of grey wool that must have been deposited by a sheep scratching its back against the rough wood. Despite its gritty, grubby appearance, the wool was soft and warm to the touch. I compressed it in my palm, closing and opening my fingers and watching it spring back to full size.

Joe looped his arm around my shoulders, pulling me closer to him.

'So go on then, Joe, spill the beans. You know you want to.'

Still watching the sheep, Joe relayed the gist of his latest conversation with Miss Harnett. They'd met at morning break, at her request.

'She was quite coquettish with me.' He smiled at the memory. 'She teased me mercilessly before announcing her verdict. "Do you happen to have an identical twin brother at home, Miss Spryke?" she asked me. "Because the governors have asked me to introduce one or two male members to our staffroom. They said we should not hasten our demise by behaving as if we're still living in the nineteenth century."'

My eyes widened. 'Goodness, the governors said that?'

Joe rested his free elbow on the top rail of the gate and rested his chin on his hand.

'That's her story,' he said. 'But you know what she's like with the governors. She calls the shots, and they agree.'

'It must be hard for her to announce a change of policy that has been a lynchpin of the school for its entire existence. It's like admitting she's been wrong all along. Presenting it to the girls' parents as the governors' request is a shrewd move.'

Joe frowned, considering.

'I'm sure that her policy was once in line with parental feeling,' he said, 'and not at all unusual. Only most other girls' schools will have moved on a few decades ago.'

'Yes, I expect so. But please, just tell me now, Joe, what was the outcome? Will you stay? Are you going to miraculously morph into Mr Spryke after half-term?'

He rubbed his nose in thought. 'It seems so. Hairnet seems comfortable with that.'

'Won't the name change be hard to explain to the girls?'

'Not these days, even at St Bride's. The school has always accepted and valued individuality. Girls and staff alike have always been encouraged to embrace their own identity and be true to themselves.'

I stepped down from the gate. My toes were starting to ache from curling them to keep my balance.

'Why do you think Hairnet's so averse to men? Is it the fallout of her unfortunate affair with Piers Galsworthy?'

Joe lowered his arm from my shoulders and took my right hand.

'Who knows? But I can't help thinking that's why Oriana's quite the opposite. Always seeking a father substitute, perhaps. Or maybe a brother.'

'Well, who wouldn't be in her position?'

Joe caught my other hand, still clenched round my tuft of sheep's wool, swung me round to face him, and bent his head to kiss me.

As we drew apart, I caught his gaze and stared into his eyes, wondering whether or not to tell him some news of my own. I could trust him, I told myself – of course I could. We began to stroll back to the car.

'Joe,' I began. 'There's something I need to speak to you about now.'

He gave my hand a reassuring squeeze.

'Not a confession of your passion for your tea companion at Doilies, I hope?'

'No, it's to do with Veronica. You see, I've been losing sleep over her little adventure ever since, beating myself up for not alerting the police to her disappearance straight after the fire drill. Honestly, I'm amazed no one else did.'

His reply made me feel even more remiss.

'Oh, but they did. I'm not sure who – maybe all of them. But Oriana told me in confidence that the police had phoned Hairnet soon after the fire drill as they'd received so many reports about a missing girl. They had to check they weren't prank calls from the pupils. This was about the same time that Max was calling the police, at Hairnet's request. And at precisely the same time, Hairnet was being alerted by the Excelsior's manager of Veronica's arrival, and they were putting safeguarding procedures in place until the arrival of her father the next day.

'She had also called Mr Thyssen and made it very clear that he must meet Veronica at Doilies at 3 p.m. the next day, without explaining the circumstances. Hairnet's methods may be a little eccentric sometimes, but she'd never risk the girls' well-being, even if it meant wrecking the school's reputation. Once the police understood she had all bases covered, they withdrew.'

I unlocked the car, and once I'd slid into the driver's seat, I gripped the steering wheel with both hands and rested my head on it.

'Now I feel even worse for not calling the police myself. I was too intent on keeping my job. I assumed we all were. I misjudged you and all my colleagues by my own poor standards.'

Joe stroked the back of my head.

'Well, I think you redeemed yourself by accepting Hairnet's mission to go to meet the supposed kidnapper. That was very brave, Gemma, and beyond the call of duty. You could have been taking a grave personal risk to save Veronica. Not that Hairnet would have put you in real danger, but you didn't know that at the time.'

I shook my head as I raised it, to stare unseeingly through the windscreen at the winding lane ahead.

'You're very generous to place such a forgiving interpretation on my behaviour, Joe. But I'm ashamed of myself for not having the courage to do what I knew in my heart to be right, out of cowardly concern for my own interests. I swear I will never put myself in that position again. And

I'm going to kick off by doing something else I should have done weeks ago.'

Joe folded his arms and gazed at me. 'And that might be?'

'I've discovered an important secret that I think will spare poor Oriana from feeling she has to throw herself at every eligible man.'

Joe raised his eyebrows expectantly.

'You know you said that Oriana suffered from not having a brother? It turns out she does have one after all. Well, a half-brother. He's been staying at the Excelsior Hotel, and now I won't rest until I've introduced them.'

34

PLAYING WITH FIRE

It hadn't been easy to persuade Oriana to leave the cosy staffroom for another wintry walk by the pond, but now that I had, she surprised me by picking up a small flat stone from the water's edge and skimming it expertly across the surface of the lake – one hop, two hops, three hops, four.

'I have to warn you, Gemma, I'm giving up men for Lent. All this business refereeing the fallout from Joe's relationship with Eleonora has made me relish a spell of singledom. Well, at least for the rest of this term.'

It was odd how the school term became the main unit of time for teachers. I'd not even been present for half a school year at St Bride's yet, but I'd already fallen into that way of thinking.

'I'm not proposing a blind date with Oliver. I just want to set you up as friends. I know the two of you will get on.'

Oriana's brow furrowed. 'So you're saying you don't think he'd fancy me?'

I sighed. 'Oh, for goodness' sake, Oriana, I'm not saying that at all.' How awkward it would be if he did. 'You said yourself that you wished you had a sibling figure in your life. There's something about Oliver that makes me think he's a made-to-measure platonic partner for you. You've so much in common.'

I hesitated, trying to build up my courage to tell her the whole truth about Oliver. Despite the chilly air, I could feel sweat starting to form along my spine. Had I said too much? I was playing with fire here, which did not bode well for a fire officer. Maybe it would be easier if I waited until he was right in front of her. I didn't want to risk her refusing to meet him.

Oriana brightened. 'So, what you mean, Gemma, is that he's charming, witty, and stylish with a rapier-sharp intellect.'

I laughed. 'If you want to put it like that, I suppose he is. He's kind too, and sensitive underneath his formal manner.'

Oriana adjusted her eau-de-Nil cashmere scarf more tightly about her neck.

'You'd better not let Joe hear you talking like that about another man, or he'll get quite the wrong impression.'

We turned away from the lake and started up the gentle incline in the direction of the main school building.

'Joe does know about him, I take it?'

'Yes. He hasn't met him yet, but I think he'd like him too. After all, you and Joe are like brother and sister, so he and Oliver are bound to get on as well.'

I bit my lip, startled at how easily these confident assertions were tripping off my tongue when I had no real proof.

'Then if this Oliver's recruiting new friends, why don't you just hook him up with Joe instead? No doubt Joe could do with some male company. It would get him out of the clutches of Max and his poker nights.'

'Oh, don't worry, I think Max has gone right off poker since this business with Veronica.'

When I held the side door open for her to enter the school building, Oriana finally conceded.

'Okay, I'll meet him, if it'll make you happy. I suppose I owe you after you've covered lessons for me. Thanks for not ratting on me to my mother, by the way. She was cross enough when I confessed to her I'd bunked off, but she forgave me soon enough when I explained my reasons: that it was the only time we could meet Joe's solicitors.' She loosened the scarf and unbuttoned her jacket. 'My mother is a very forgiving person, you know.'

I needed to hear that. I hoped introducing Oriana to her half-brother wasn't about to lose me my job, but I'd already decided I'd rather do that than stand by and watch Oliver slip out of Oriana's life before he'd even entered it.

35

SHAKESPEAREAN TWINS

'I suppose this Oliver must be quite posh to be staying at the Excelsior,' said Joe, peering out of the window from the passenger seat as I reversed into a tight parking space on the hotel forecourt. It was the exeat weekend and we'd opted to spend it in school together. I'd arranged for us to meet Oliver for lunch on the Saturday, and he'd arranged to stay the weekend in Cirencester.

'Or affluent, at least,' Oriana added.

Perhaps the old Oriana wasn't so far beneath the surface after all.

She scooted over to sit in the middle of the back seat and leaned forward to reapply a neutral lipstick with the aid of my rear-view mirror.

'I suppose he might have independent means,' I replied. 'Plus he's here on business to research a book, so he'll probably be able to offset the hotel bill against tax.'

'Well, I don't care how rich he is, I'm paying my way to make it clear this is not a date,' Oriana said.

To lure Oliver back to the Cotswolds so soon, I'd emailed to tell him I had more material relating to his father that I could only pass on to him in person. I counted Oriana as material, although not the kind he might have been expecting.

To salve my conscience for this white lie, I'd wheedled out of Judith the loan of a guestbook from the era when Piers Galsworthy was chairman of governors, showing the precise times and dates of his trips to the school and the purpose of each visit. In those days there was no security officer to safeguard the estate and the girls. Hairnet had appointed Max just a few years before my arrival. The only formal show of security in those days was that visitors had to sign in at reception on arrival.

When we reached Doilies, Oliver was already seated at a round corner table, three quarters of it surrounded by a high-backed red velvet padded banquette. Seeing I'd brought two guests with me, he slid around to the centre of the banquette to make room.

'Hello, Gemma, how lovely to see you again.' His eyes darted immediately to the cracked chestnut leather-bound book under my arm. 'That looks interesting.'

I took a seat beside him, and Joe gave a sharp intake of breath as Oliver leaned forward to kiss me on both cheeks. I set the book on the other side of me, to stop Oliver diving into it straight away.

'I hope you don't mind that I've brought my colleagues Joe Spryke and Oriana Bliss with me? It's exeat weekend, so it's a rare chance for us all to go out to lunch together.'

'Of course not. It's a pleasure to meet you Oriana, Joe. In fact, a pleasure to meet anyone connected with St Bride's. Gemma here has been the only one at the school who's been kind enough to respond to my enquiries. I presume she's told you of the reason for my interest in the school?'

Immediately my pulse started to race as the enormity of what I was doing began to dawn on me. I really hadn't thought this through.

'I've told them you're writing a biography of Piers Galsworthy. That you're a writer. That's all.'

I didn't dare look at Oriana, who had sat on the chair opposite Oliver. Oliver glanced from Oriana to Joe.

'Of course, you're far too young to have known my father. Still, it's nice to meet you. Kind of you to take an interest.'

He shifted on the bench seat to peer over my lap at the visitors' book.

'So, I presume this is the new material you mentioned?' he asked.

I pushed the cutlery and serviettes aside to clear enough space to open the book on the table in front of me.

'Yes, that's right. It's a record of all Piers Galsworthy's visits to St Bride's, from his first appointment to the board until the formal closure of the charity. I thought you'd like to see it and take notes for your book. I can leave it with you overnight and collect it from you tomorrow before you check out. But please be careful with it. It's not really meant to be removed from the school premises.'

I'd intended that he should only look at the book after we'd gone, as there wasn't really much in it of relevance to his research, but he was so keen for new evidence of his father that he immediately began to flip over the pages. He used his fingertips, with the delicacy and respect of a museum curator touching an invaluable, ancient artefact. It would not have surprised me to see him pull a pair of archivist's white cotton gloves from his pocket and put them on.

'Interesting to see how much his handwriting changes from one visit to the next.' Slowly Oliver turned the pages. 'As if he came in very different frames of mind, according to whom he was meeting, whether for board meetings, for school events or for one-to-one meetings with the headmistress.'

I swallowed. I hadn't noticed that.

'Of course, I'd expect his handwriting to deteriorate in the last few months, when he didn't have long to live,' said Oliver. 'Although I don't believe he knew he had a terminal illness before he died – his devastating heart attack was sudden and fatal. Look, his writing's very spidery here.'

Oriana leaned across the table to see.

'That's my birthday,' she murmured.

Oliver smiled politely but was not diverted from his own line of thinking.

'You see, my mother never liked to speak of him, which is why I know so painfully little about him. That's why I had to contact St Bride's in the first place.'

'What has your mother got to do with Piers Galsworthy? Was your sister a pupil here?' Oriana's eyes widened, and Joe shifted in his seat.

'No, I haven't any sisters, nor brothers either. That's why this project means far more to me than the sort of commissioned biography that I usually write. You see, Piers Galsworthy was my father. He died when I was a baby, so I never knew him. My mother remarried soon afterwards to a perfectly decent man who brought me up as his own. Since my step-father died a few years ago and my mother died last year, I'm finally able to get to know my biological father without upsetting them.'

Oriana clasped her hands on the table in front of her, straightened her back, and gazed evenly at Oliver, the picture of control. But when she spoke there was a catch in her throat.

'Oliver, I also would be very interested to find out more about him. You see, Piers Galsworthy was my father too.'

Oliver's jaw dropped. 'So I do have a sibling after all. At least, a half-sister.'

He seemed to recover from the initial shock and gave a genuine, heartfelt smile.

'How wonderful,' he said. 'I cannot tell you how glad that makes me.' He laid a hand on his chest in a gesture characteristic of Oriana. She immediately did the same, reminding me of an exercise I'd seen the girls do in pairs in a drama lesson, where one must mirror the other's actions.

Oliver lowered his eyes to the book once more, and I realised he was gazing at the date when his father's handwriting looked particularly shaky.

'You said your birthday is three months before mine. I'm guessing you must be quite a bit older than me, then, because my parents were married for some years before I came along. I suppose it's not impossible that my father had been married before, but if so, why wasn't it mentioned in his obituary?'

He gazed at Oriana for a moment.

'I have to say, you must have taken very good care of yourself, as you certainly don't look any older than me. And now I look at you, I realise how many similarities there are between us, not just in looks but in mannerisms too. How very strange. We're more like whole siblings than half; we could even be twins.'

I made a feeble attempt to lighten the mood. 'How very Shake-spearean all this is.'

They each gave me an oddly similar funny look.

Oriana's fingers fluttered to her mouth.

'Just how old are you, Oliver?'

'I'm thirty.'

'So am I. I'm afraid the reason you didn't know about Piers Galsworthy's prior marriage is that there wasn't one. He became my father while he was married to your mother, but not to mine.'

They fell silent, as they stared at each other with the same slightly downturned, golden-coloured eyes. Joe coughed and drew back his chair.

'I think we could all do with a cup of tea. What does one have to do to get a cup of tea in this place?' When he turned to look for a waitress, he found himself looking up into the astonished faces of Hairnet and the bursar.

36

A FAMILY TEA

'Mother!' cried Oriana, leaping to her feet.

When Hairnet, usually so poised, staggered slightly, Joe got up and helped her into his chair. The bursar, focused only on Hairnet, knelt beside her and reached for her hand.

'Caroline, are you okay?'

Still holding on to her, he panned the room for the waitress and waved his free hand for her attention. Sensing his agitation, the waitress excused herself from serving a customer at a table on the other side of the room and rushed over to ours.

'A glass of water for the lady please. And tea, strong tea, at once.'

The waitress looked around at us all expectantly, perhaps sensing the drama of the moment.

'For six? Is that tea for six?'

'Yes please,' said Oliver, and for a moment I thought the bursar had spoken without moving his lips.

The conversation had given Hairnet the chance to regain some of her usual composure.

'I'm so sorry, my dears, it's just that this gentleman reminds me so much of an old friend that seeing you together quite shook me up for a moment. But of course, now I realise he is just Gemma's friend.' She turned to me. 'So, my dear, is this a double date? I seem to recognise this gentleman. He is the one with the elegant car, is he not? Thank you so much for taking up my suggestion of introducing them.'

Oliver, ever polite, beamed at them across the table.

'Hello, I'm so pleased to meet you. I recognise your faces from the school prospectus, which makes me feel as if I know you already. Miss Harnett, Mr Marshall.' He smiled at them each in turn, presumably anticipating they might have a lot more to tell him about his late father than I could. 'But I have you at a disadvantage. You don't know who I am. Please allow me to introduce myself. I'm Oliver Galsworthy.'

When he stood up to shake their hands across the table, Hairnet slumped back in her seat, dropping her hands to her lap.

'Galsworthy, you say? Oliver Galsworthy? My dear, that puts a very different complexion on the matter. Oriana, Gemma, really!'

She turned to us, helpless.

Oriana raised her eyes to the ceiling as if she might find a handy hint there on how to deal with awkward family revelations, before she replied.

'You know what they say, Mother, you can choose your friends, but you can't choose your family.'

Hairnet stared blankly at the place setting in front of her.

'So, the time has come at last,' she said. 'I'm so sorry, Oriana, I never intended for you to meet Oliver this way, if at all. When you were very young, I fondly imagined introducing you to your half-brother when you were both old enough to understand the situation. I hoped you might get on swimmingly, in spite of – well, in spite of everything. But you grew up too quickly, his mother rebuffed my advances, and the right moment passed – gone forever, I thought.' Eyes bright with unshed tears, she offered both hands now to Oriana, but Oriana kept hers tightly clasped on the snowy tablecloth.

The waitress returned bearing a laden tray and looked from one of us to the other for guidance.

'A glass of water for the lady and tea for six?'

Joe hurried to clear enough space on the table for the enormous tea pot, flask of hot water, milk jug, and tea strainer, and I closed the guest-book, sliding it off the table and on to my lap.

Hairnet held her glass of water to her lips and took several sips, letting each roll around her mouth, as if to rehydrate it by absorption rather than swallowing.

To buy everyone thinking time, I raised the enormous teapot, my wrist almost buckling under its weight.

'Shall I be mother?' I said brightly, then nearly dropped the teapot at the crassness of my remark.

To my relief, Hairnet smiled in amusement.

'Now that would be a surprise,' she said.

37

PIERS' LEGACY

Oriana bowed her head.

'I have so many questions, Mother, and I'm sure Oliver does too. I think you owe us both an explanation.'

She looked up and gazed at Oliver while the rest of us offered each other the milk jug, with the same formal courtesy I'd become used to in the Trough.

Oriana continued. 'You know, even if no one had told me, I think if I'd met you by chance, I'd have sensed a connection between us. We look so alike. If you were a girl, I might have taken you for a doppelganger and dropped dead.'

Miss Harnett pressed a hand to her heart. 'Please don't say that, even in jest, my dear.'

When Oliver smiled at Oriana, his lips took the same shape as hers, sans lip gloss.

As we stirred our tea, Hairnet gathered her thoughts.

'My dears, in a way I am glad to get the matter out in the open at last, although I'd never pictured it happening quite like this.' She glanced around the room at the expensive toile de Jouy wallpaper and the cream lace curtains. 'Though I must say this is a very agreeable setting for your first meeting after thirty years of secrecy.'

Oriana set down her cup. 'It's hardly a secret, Mother. I mean, the bursar, Joe, and Gemma all know that I'm your daughter, and it wouldn't surprise me if other staff had guessed, although they're too polite to admit it. God, we're all so British about it. Our reserve has even rubbed off on Nicolette.'

The bursar opened his mouth to speak, but Miss Harnett laid a hand on his arm to stop him. She allowed Oriana to continue.

'If you think I've never googled Piers Galsworthy or checked out the school archives and read his obituary – which mentions and names his son – you're sadly mistaken. And did you really think you could hide from me the fact that he was in the neighbourhood, researching his father's biography, by cutting out those articles from the local paper? Didn't you think I'd hear about it from somewhere else? I've had at least three people, including my hairdresser, tell me they'd been reading about it in the local paper last week. Not that they realised my connection with him of course, but in this digital age, you can't muffle facts so easily.'

She paused for breath, but she clearly wasn't done yet, so no one dared interrupt.

'Honestly, it's been more embarrassing to have my colleagues in the staffroom afraid to mention it for fear of stirring up trouble than to have it openly discussed. Of course, I've known for years that I had a half-brother called Oliver, but I've never tried to track him down for fear of hurting you, Mother. To be honest' – she gazed down into her teacup – 'I'd assumed that if I ever tried to find him at all, it would have to be after your death. But I could cope with that, even if it meant not meeting Oliver until we were both in our dotage. After all, I've lived without him for thirty years. Besides, I might not even like him. If allowing you to believe I knew nothing about him made it easier for you to live with your past, I was prepared to go along with it. You come first for me, Mother. Nothing will ever change that.'

We were all silent, our eyes on Hairnet, awaiting her reaction, which quickly followed.

'Actually, Oriana, it wasn't that secret I was talking about. Geoffrey, I think the time has come.'

She drank a little tea, probably wishing there was a fortifying drop of sherry in it.

'First, promise me you will all keep what I'm about to tell you to yourselves until you go to your graves. Or at least until I tell you otherwise. If any of this got into the press, it would surely be the end of St Bride's.'

We gazed at each wide-eyed, wondering what on earth she was about to reveal.

'You see, Oriana, I'm afraid Piers Galsworthy wasn't actually your father.'

'What?' Oriana's hands flew to her cheeks so fast that she knocked her teaspoon on to the floor. No one bothered to pick it up. 'Then why did he transfer ownership of the school to you? I thought it was some kind of alimony, or whatever you'd call it considering you weren't married. Child maintenance, perhaps.'

Oliver looked from mother to daughter in puzzlement before the bursar came to his rescue, after receiving Hairnet's nod of approval. He cleared his throat.

'Just over thirty years ago, Piers Galsworthy had a short affair with Caroline – with Miss Harnett – during which she discovered she was expecting Oriana. He would not leave his wife, but he was determined to provide for Caroline and her unborn child for the rest of their lives. So he arranged a little business transfer that would ensure her financial security. The St Bride's estate became her personal property and her responsibility. The charity running the school had been doing a poor job of it for some time, so on the surface it was a reasonable business arrangement. Caroline had to present a proposal whereby she'd run the school more effectively as a private individual, but still within the specifications laid down by Lord Bunting. Which indeed she did.'

'With your help, Geoffrey. I couldn't have done it without you.'

The bursar gave a modest nod, then sat back.

Oliver spoke slowly. 'You said just now my mother knew about your baby. About Oriana.'

Hairnet and the bursar looked at each other for a moment, before Hairnet spoke.

'Yes, and at first it perplexed her, because tests had shown some years before that Piers Galsworthy was unable to father children, as the unfortunate consequence of a severe dose of mumps in his early twenties. There was no vaccine for mumps when we were children.'

Oliver had clasped his hands on the table, and his knuckles were beginning to pale. Both he and Oriana had slender, tapering fingers, all the more similar for Oriana leaving off her customary nail polish.

Oriana gulped. 'So Piers Galsworthy couldn't have been my father after all?'

Oliver closed his eyes. 'And if he was sterile, he couldn't have been mine either. That explains why I don't look remotely like him.'

When he opened his eyes, he was staring at the bursar. The same chestnut eyes stared back at him from beneath the same neat, sandy eyebrows.

The bursar moved one hand across the table to within touching distance of Miss Harnett's.

'Caroline, I think Oliver may have guessed.'

She laid her hand over his and gave it a gentle squeeze of encouragement.

'My dears,' she said, 'it is true that you are half-siblings, but not because you share a father in Piers Galsworthy. Oliver, Oriana, may I introduce your biological father? Geoffrey Marshall is the father of you both.'

'But how?' Oriana clapped her hand across her mouth. 'No, I don't mean how. Please spare us the graphic details. Respect a daughter's sensibilities. I mean how come Piers Galsworthy acted as if you were carrying his child? He must have known he was sterile.'

'Oh, he knew all right. But Geoffrey wasn't. My dears, it shames me to confess, but I'd broken off a much longer affair with Geoffrey after a silly tiff and allowed Piers Galsworthy to seduce me on the rebound.' She turned to Oliver. 'He was a charming, handsome man, especially fond of female company, and he rather took advantage of his medical condition. Knowing he could play the field without leaving a trail of babies in his wake, he allowed himself to do what he pleased. On the surface, he seemed to have it all: wealth, a successful and prestigious career, a devoted wife. But beneath the glittering façade, as well as the secret string of lovers, of which I was just one, lurked one great sorrow: that he couldn't give your mother a child. He loved her very much, you can be sure of that.

'Our affair didn't last long, and I quickly realised that Oriana had been conceived before it had really begun. Oliver, when your mother found out what had happened, she made a beeline for Geoffrey, seducing him with the sole intention of conceiving a child by him. A child she'd then pass off as Piers Galsworthy's.'

'Oh, Bursar, you...!' Oriana was ready to be outraged, but then gave a hollow laugh. 'I'm sorry, but I don't think I can stop calling you Bursar.'

She gave an awkward grin, but her eyes were bright with tears.

Oliver seemed less forgiving. 'But Bursar, how could you do that, knowing Caroline was already expecting your baby? How could you possibly...?'

When the bursar looked down in silence, Hairnet came to his defence.

'Oliver, Geoffrey didn't know I was expecting. Only Piers did. I didn't tell Geoffrey until much later when I could no longer hide it. I was so angry and jealous when I discovered he'd become involved with your mother, I wanted nothing more to do with him. But of course, we had to continue to work together, especially when the school was transferred into my ownership. I needed his safe pair of hands on the school's finances and the management of the estate, and he needed his job and his tied house.'

'Of course, there was another reason I stayed at St Bride's,' said the bursar quietly, gazing at Hairnet with unmistakable adoration.

Hairnet reached out to take his hand. 'I can tell you that although it took many, many years, I found it in my heart to forgive Geoffrey; our relationship has recently, shall we say, become rather warmer.'

Oriana put her fingers in her ears. 'Too much information, Mother.'

Then she let her hands drop quickly to her lap, where she laced her fingers tightly together, her knuckles whitening.

'But why in all this time have you never thought to tell me he is my father? Why not? Why ever not? Surely I have a right to know, especially when he's always been more or less under the same roof as me, mostly within spitting distance.'

Oriana's face crumpled with rage as she turned to the bursar, who recoiled slightly, perhaps fearing she might spit at him right now.

The poor man shook his head sadly. 'And break my promise to your mother, and risk driving her even further away from me? No. I had always hoped for a reconciliation, no matter how long it might take.'

Hairnet raised her hand as if to deflect Oriana's wrath from the bursar.

'The blame lies entirely with me, Oriana. *Mea culpa.* I allowed myself to put my career before the emotional needs of my child. Having accepted ownership of St Bride's and responsibility for its management, I was afraid that if I made your parentage public knowledge, the school would somehow be taken away from me, as I had effectively gained possession under false pretences.'

Hairnet unfolded the snowy linen serviette beside her tea plate and dabbed at the corners of her eyes.

'My goodness, if any of you thought less of Mr Thyssen for seeming to pay more attention to his business than to his daughter, what must you think of me now? I am guilty of an unspeakable lapse in my duty of care to you, dear Oriana.'

Seeing the tears streaming freely now down Hairnet's face, Oriana's expression softened.

'Mother, you've always shown me nothing but love,' she said gently. 'Never let it be said that you've neglected me. Besides, no-one can take St Bride's away from you now, can they? Not after all those goings-on at the end of last term.'

She turned to the bursar for moral support.

'Know this, Oriana,' the bursar continued, emboldened now by being the centre of attention for once. 'I have also always loved you like a daughter – as a daughter, rather... my daughter. I am just thankful to have been near you as you grew up. I only wish I'd been able to spend as much time in Oliver's company. But not with his mother, of course. No offence, Oliver.'

The bursar glanced nervously at Hairnet, but she just nodded approval. She had to clear her throat before she could speak.

'Oliver, I must tell you, as perhaps the person most short-changed in all our tangled dealings, Piers Galsworthy loved you as much as if you were his natural son for the few months that he knew you, and he always took good care of your mother, despite his open marriage. He left her well provided for, as he did me. In his own way, he was a decent man, a kind and caring man, as well as a shrewd and gifted businessman.'

'The bursar is too,' added Oriana, the tension on her face beginning to fade.

The bursar's mouth fell open.

'He's been devoted to my mother and to St Bride's, you know.'

The bursar gave a little squeak of surprise.

'He's always looked out for me too,' Oriana continued. 'I've always wondered why, when I've often been a little short with him.' That was an understatement, but we all let that go unchecked. 'I'm sorry, Bursar, for the times I've been ungracious and ungrateful.'

'What about the business with the Bolivars?' he replied, apparently unable to take in her changed attitude. 'When I caused you to lose all that money?'

Oriana shook her head. 'I shouldn't have been so stupid to go after that dreadful Venezuelan guy in the first place. I'll try to be kinder to you in the future, Bursar. I'll do my best – I can promise you that. It's going to feel awfully weird, though, knowing that you are my father, but I suppose I could do a lot worse.' She gave a little laugh. 'I mean, for a start, you've got a pulse.'

Then her hand flew to her mouth. 'I'm sorry Oliver, I didn't mean...'

For once she couldn't finish her sentence.

Oliver just smiled and shook his head to dismiss her concern.

Joe had been watching Oliver while Oriana was talking.

'It must be disconcerting for you, Oliver,' he began, 'after researching what you thought was your father's biography, only to find you've been following the wrong man entirely.'

Oliver scratched his head. 'Well, Piers Galsworthy is still an interesting

person, even though it's much nicer to know that my real father is still alive.'
He smiled shyly at the bursar. 'I think if nobody would mind, though, I
might finish the book regardless,' he added. 'It seems a shame to let all that
work go to waste. It may be of interest to a publisher of business books.'

The bursar put his head in his hands. 'Oliver, I'm afraid my life story
isn't half as impressive as Piers Galsworthy's, and no one will ever want to
write my biography. But if you ever feel you might want to get to know me
at all, I'm here for you. I don't know if you can understand how hard it
was for me to ignore the emails you sent me last term asking for help
with your research. Believe me, I longed to say yes so that I could meet
you at last. The first time I saw your photograph in one of those articles
the local paper has been running since Christmas, about how you were
seeking people in this area who might have known Piers Galsworthy, I
thought for a moment it was a picture of myself in my younger days. I'm
so pleased to be able to meet you in the flesh at last, even if you never
want to see me again.'

As Oliver gazed at the bursar for a moment, the corners of his mouth
twitched in amusement.

'So you are what I'll look like in thirty years' time, are you?'

'Ooh, just like Dorian Gray and his portrait in the attic,' I said lightly,
trying to ease the tension.

'That's no bad thing,' said Miss Harnett briskly, but her eyes were
gentle. 'Now, I propose we make the best of this muddle by turning it into
a celebration. Who would like to sample some of the legendary chocolate
cake that so enthralled Veronica Thyssen?'

A few minutes later, the waitress was unloading six delicate bone-
china plates from her trolley, one in front of each of us.

'So it was you who cut those articles out of the staffroom copies of the
local paper?' I asked the bursar as the waitress set down a plate of cake
beside the teapot.

The bursar held up his hand. 'Guilty as charged. I was tempted not to
put the papers in the staffroom at all for fear of inciting questions about
the missing articles, but then I reasoned that whichever member of staff
was next in a newsagent would just buy another copy for the staffroom
and give the game away. I crossed my fingers that you'd all assume one of

your colleagues had snipped out a story to use in the classroom for a lesson.'

I covered my eyes with my hands. 'And there was me terrified that the missing articles were the work of some paparazzi in pursuit of you, Joe!'

Oliver straightened his back. 'Really, Joe? Do you also have some sort of scandal in your past? Join the club!'

It wasn't that funny, but we needed to laugh, so we did. When I helped myself to a slice of chocolate cake, I realised I'd been terribly hungry.

38

BENEATH THE PLINTH

Before the afternoon was over, Hairnet telephoned me in my flat, where I'd gone to read quietly before joining Joe for supper at the Bluebird. Oriana was returning to the Excelsior for dinner with Oliver. They seemed to be getting on rather well, cautious of each other's feelings but finding common ground besides their shared genes.

Hairnet asked me to meet her in her study. Her voice sounded calm and steady, but when I entered, her face was flushed and her eyes were pink. On the way down the stairs, I'd convinced myself she was about to fire me for gross misconduct, because without my aiding and abetting Oliver, her thirty-year secret would still be intact.

As I took a seat on the sofa opposite her desk, McPhee trotted across the Persian carpet to rub his chin against my ankles.

'So, Miss Lamb.'

My stomach flipped at this uncharacteristically formal address. When she hesitated, I fell into the trap of rushing to fill the void.

'Miss Harnett, I am so sorry. I've intervened in something that was none of my business. I've caused hurt and embarrassment to you and the bursar and Oriana and Oliver. I cannot begin to imagine how difficult it will be for them to process today's revelations, or to come to terms with them. They must now be wondering who they are, after spending their lifetime hankering after the wrong father.'

With a chirrup, McPhee jumped on to my lap and I allowed him to curl up into a tight ball of black fur.

Hairnet pushed back her chair and got to her feet, before strolling over to the window to gaze at the lawn dotted with tight crocus flowers in mauve, white, and gold. Five o'clock and it was not yet quite dark: spring was on its way at last. I assumed she couldn't bring herself to look at me while she gave me my marching orders.

'Actually, Gemma, I'm rather impressed. You did what you thought was right without regard for your own well-being, introducing Oriana to the sibling she longed for. You could not have known the enormity of the beast you were unleashing, but perhaps it's better that Oriana knows the truth now than finding out only after I am gone, when I'm not here to tell her my version and to reassure her that she is loved and was always very much wanted. Now her real father can openly express his love too, if she will accept it.'

'Oh, I think she will.'

As we'd been leaving Doilies and returning to our cars, I'd noticed Oriana slip one arm through the bursar's and the other through her mother's and walk in step with them to the car park. Joe and I had driven back to St Bride's in my car while Oriana rode with her parents.

'You put the happiness of others before your own,' she continued.

I kept stroking McPhee, scarcely daring to believe that I wouldn't be leaving the room unemployed and homeless.

'Which I should have done myself years ago.' She sighed and turned back to face me. 'Perhaps if her other sibling had survived, she would not have felt so lonely.'

'Her other sibling?' I'd never imagined there was a third child involved.

'Oriana was one of twins. A second baby girl was stillborn. Laurel lies buried in the second plinth in the mausoleum.'

'The second plinth? Along with Piers Galsworthy?'

Rumour had it that Galsworthy was buried there, which was why Hairnet had the bizarre habit of going to lie down on it to think.

'Oh goodness, no. He's buried at his family's local church. No, little Laurel lies beneath the plinth, and sometimes I just need to be near her and think what might have been.'

'Laurel. What a pretty name.'

'Yes, chosen to match Olive, which as you know is Oriana's real name. In my youth, I was a keen student of Greek history and culture.'

Digging his claws into my thighs for traction, McPhee jumped off my lap and padded over to the feet of his mistress. She scooped him up in her arms and held him close to her chest.

'Yes, and you may imagine how enraged I was when Piers' wife chose to call her son Oliver. It felt as if she was stealing my surviving daughter's identity. It was a relief in a way when in her teens she decided to rename herself Oriana. And to dye her hair too, which, depending on her chosen colour, often made her look much less like her father. Frankly I've always thought the bursar a handsome fellow.' She let out a nervous little laugh. 'Like father, like son, eh? But I digress. Will you join me in a sherry, my dear? I'm rather feeling the need.'

So was I.

Emboldened by the first sip, I had one last question to ask Hairnet.

'So have you ever told Oriana about Laurel?'

For a moment, Hairnet froze, the glass halfway to her lips. When McPhee jumped on to her lap and began to purr, she allowed herself a self-deprecating smile.

'My dear, one day perhaps I will.'

39

CREATIVE INTENTIONS FULFILLED

Joe was helping me mount the girls' baby photographs on the boards that had been set up on the library tables. The display would provide a party game at the Valentine's Ball – a new event on the school calendar to which all the girls and their parents were invited. Following an emergency governors' meeting, Hairnet would use the occasion to announce a change in school policy, allowing for the employment of male teachers.

When she had written beforehand to the girls' parents outlining the proposal, to her surprise and to Joe's relief (and mine), not a single one had objected. Some had expressed enthusiasm and even congratulations.

'Look at this picture, Joe. I bet this is Veronica and her mother.'

He took the snapshot of a strangely familiar dark-haired woman, holding a toddler in a pink party dress. He flipped it over to read the label on the back.

'Yep, you're right.' He turned it back over to examine it more closely. 'Gosh, it's like looking at Veronica in twenty years' time. You can see a resemblance between mother and toddler in the picture, but it's much stronger now Veronica's older. I bet her mother looked exactly like her as a teenager.'

He picked up a couple of drawing pins from the pot on the table and added the photo to the display board in a space between two older pupils' pictures. We were mixing up the year groups to make it harder for everyone to guess who was who. I straightened the photo beside it, whose drawing pin had become dislodged.

'Veronica told me how much she looks like her late mother,' I said. 'She was worried that was why her father was reluctant to spend more time with her. It made him too sad. Not that it's any excuse. Veronica needed him all the more to fill the void in her own life.' I reached for the last of what had been a pile of a hundred baby photos. 'With any luck, his new girlfriend will help him move on. Or new fiancée, I should say. Veronica seems to like her future stepmother a lot, and from what I can gather, she seems to have the measure of Veronica. She's stopped Mr Thyssen sending these ridiculously extravagant Harrods parcels every week, and makes him send a lovely greeting card instead, including a handwritten note. Not a lengthy missive – he's still a busy man, as we know, and I don't suppose pouring his heart out to his daughter comes naturally to him after all these years of reticence and restraint – but enough to show her he loves her. Veronica's pinning all his cards above her bed. I'm so pleased for her, and for him – for their family.'

'Presumably he'll bring his fiancée to the Valentine's Ball tonight?'

I nodded. 'Yes, I think he will. After all those shenanigans after missing the start-of-term tea party at Doilies, I think Hairnet gave him an invitation he couldn't refuse.'

'Quite right too.'

'And speaking of changes, are you going to change your surname back to your real name, the one you were known by as a professional cyclist? You can drop your disguise entirely now.'

Joe bit his lip. 'Nah. I've grown quite fond of Spryke. Rhymes with bike. What's not to love? Besides, it's my mother's maiden name. It's still part of who I am.'

I couldn't disagree.

We stood back to admire our handiwork. The girls were going to have great fun identifying each other, and the bursar had stumped up a highly desirable prize for the girl able to correctly identify the most babies: an instant Polaroid camera with film to create new memories. Each of the girls would also find a disposable camera at her place setting that night to capture the fun of the Ball.

Joe glanced at the clock on the wall. 'I'd better dash if I'm to make my barber's appointment.' He was due to appear at the Ball in his new persona as next term's PE teacher, Mr Spryke – though in truth it would not be very different at all.

I reached up to pull playfully at his golden curls.

'I think I'm going to miss these,' I said.

He shook his head to fend off my fingers. 'I won't. They don't half slow me down on my bike.'

'Even though you always wear a crash helmet?'

He gave a sheepish grin. 'Well, maybe it's all in the mind. Still, it's on the critical path to achieving my creative intention for the term.'

I put my finger to my lips.

'Don't tell Hairnet,' I said, 'but I never got round to writing mine down.'

'Well, while I'm at the barber's, I give you permission to take my statement out of my pigeonhole – remember, that I stashed at the start of term? – and read it. But for now, I must fly.'

Giving me a chaste kiss on the top of my head, he marched out of the library and headed for the bike shed.

I replaced the lid on the plastic pot of drawing pins and returned them to Mavis's desk at the far end of the library. Then I sauntered off to the staffroom.

There were no lessons for the rest of the day to allow the girls more time to get ready for the Ball. As I passed Veronica in the entrance hall, she waved to me, smiling with childish pleasure as, with a gaggle of other Year 7s, she inflated pearlescent, heart-shaped, red balloons. Sixth formers were on stand-by, ready to hoist the balloons into a net above the dance floor for release at the end of the evening. Veronica was smiling all the time these days. Hairnet might have to rethink her Most Inscrutable award for Speech Day. Perhaps it should be Widest Smile instead.

The staffroom was empty, and for once I was glad of the privacy as I retrieved Joe's tiny note from his pigeonhole. With my fingernail I peeled back the sticky tape that had sealed in its secret. I unfolded the paper to reveal just two words:

Be myself.

I gazed at it for a moment before refolding it and slipping it into my jacket pocket.

I wished I'd thought to make the same pledge at the start of term. But my omission didn't matter. Even without the conscious intention, I'd managed to achieve the same goal. I'd been true to myself in the end, standing up for what I believed in, even though I'd known it might cost me my job. Another term, another lesson learned. I couldn't wait to see what the next term would bring me – including Mr Spryke.

ACKNOWLEDGMENTS

With grateful thanks to all those who helped, directly or indirectly, with the writing of this book:

Friends, former colleagues, and past pupils of Westonbirt School, where I worked for thirteen years in rather different circumstances from Gemma Lamb's. It's an entirely different kind of school to the fictitious St Bride's, but the strength and warmth of its community spirit inspired me to invent St Bride's.

Victoria Coren Mitchell for giving me insights into the mind of the poker player in her fascinating memoir, *For Richer, For Poorer: Confessions of a Player*.

My author friend Rachel Harrison for reminding me of the source of the Lord Peter Wimsey quote about the difficulty of disguising a back.

My ever patient and supportive daughter Laura for typing my hand-written manuscript and processing my numerous scribbled edits.

The brilliant Rachel Lawston for her cover design for this new edition from Boldwood Books.

The wonderful Boldwood Books team: Amanda Ridout, Tara Loder, Sue Lamprell, Madeleine Hamey-Thomas, Emily Reader, Jenna Houston, and Nia Beynon for their expertise, hard work and faith in me, in Gemma Lamb, and St Bride's.

Debbie Young

MORE FROM DEBBIE YOUNG

We hope you enjoyed reading *Wicked Whispers at St Bride's*. If you did, please leave a review.

If you'd like to gift a copy, this book is also available as an ebook, digital audio download and audiobook CD.

Sign up to Debbie Youngs' mailing list for news, competitions and updates on future books.

https://bit.ly/DebbieYoungNews

The first in the Gemma Lamb Cozy Mystery series, *Dastardly Deeds at St Bride's*, is available now.

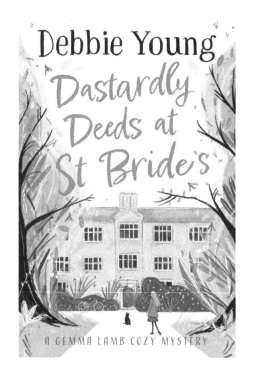

Debbie Young

Dastardly
Deeds at
St Bride's

A GEMMA LAMB COZY MYSTERY

ABOUT THE AUTHOR

Debbie Young is the much-loved author of the Sophie Sayers and St Brides cosy crime mysteries. She lives in a Cotswold village, where she runs the local literary festival, and has worked at Westonbirt School, both of which provide inspiration for her writing.

Visit Debbie's Website: www.authordebbieyoung.com.

facebook.com/AuthorDebbieYoung

instagram.com/debbieyoungauthor

bookbub.com/authors/debbie-young

twitter.com/DebbieYoungBN

Boldw👁👁d

Boldwood Books is an award-winning fiction publishing company seeking out the best stories from around the world.

Find out more at www.boldwoodbooks.com

Join our reader community for brilliant books, competitions and offers!

Follow us
@BoldwoodBooks
@BookandTonic

Sign up to our weekly deals newsletter

https://bit.ly/BoldwoodBNewsletter